THE SNOW LEOPARD'S LOVE

HARMONY RAINES

The Snow Leopard's Love

The Bond of Brothers

Book Five

* * *

Sign up to the Harmony Raines Newsletter by going to:
http://www.harmonyraines.com/newsletter-sign-up/
Never miss a new release!
You'll also receive the EBOOK *'A Bond to Bear'*
Just to say thank you!

SERIES ORDER

1. The White Wolf of Wishing Moon Bay
2. The Horse Shifter's Mate
3. Her Fae-vorite Bear
4. Fae-ted to the Bear

5. The Snow Leopard's Love

6. The Dragon Shifter's Desire

US LINKS

Website and Newsletter: harmonyraines.com

Facebook: facebook.com/harmonyrainesauthor

Amazon Author Page: amazon.com/Harmony-Raines/e/B0090Q3DWM

Bond of Brothers Series Page

On Amazon: amazon.com/dp/B08T6JF1QZ

On My Website: harmonyraines.com/all-books/bond-of-brothers-series

UK LINKS

Website and Newsletter: harmonyraines.com

Facebook: facebook.com/harmonyrainesauthor

Amazon Author Page: amazon.co.uk/Harmony-Raines/e/B0090Q3DWM

Bond of Brothers Series Page

On Amazon: amazon.co.uk/dp/B08T6JF1QZ

On My Website: harmonyraines.com/all-books/bond-of-brothers-series

THE SNOW LEOPARD'S LOVE

THE BOND OF BROTHERS

Book Five

A silverback shifter romance

Belle is done with men. Her husband left her and their children for another woman and never looked back. All she knows about her father is that he was a bad man who wound up dead because of his bad ways.

So why does she feel compelled to trust the man in front of her? A man who is obviously lying when he says he's a snow leopard shifter.

There's no such thing as shifters. Just like there's no such thing as true love.

Belle's about to discover she's *wrong* about a lot of things.

She's also about to learn that Rift is the *right* one for her.

Rift has found his mate, at last. But Belle doesn't want anything to do with him.

Somehow, he must persuade her that they're meant to be

together *forever*. However, she wants him to turn around and walk straight back out of her life.

It's what she wants. He can see it in her eyes.

What's a shifter to do?

When Belle and her family are threatened, Rift is the one, she calls on for help. He grabs the opportunity to show her what being a shifter's mate is all about.

But a new discovery threatens the safety of not just Belle's family, but Rift's too.

1

BELLE

"I'd like you all to get back in your truck and drive away." Belle's even voice didn't betray her fear as she faced down the group of strangers who had arrived at her dead uncle's house. Reggie had caused trouble all his life, any hope that had ended with his death was fading fast.

They should have gotten someone else to come and empty the house. However, Belle's mom, Katrina, had hoped that emptying the rented house of her brother's possessions might give them some kind of closure.

Belle suspected her mom also hoped to find some evidence that Reggie cared for his family, or at least thought of them in some small way. So far there had been no evidence of that. Not one single photo of his family.

She gnawed her bottom lip. She shouldn't have brought the children with her. Jack and Rosie should have been shielded from any connection with Reggie, who had never done a good deed in his whole life. At least according to Katrina.

But Belle had brought them.

Smart move, Belle told herself as she faced the five

strangers in front of her. She'd put her children in danger. Something she swore she would never do.

"We aren't looking for trouble." The first guy out of the truck had gotten as far as the gate before whatever drug he was on took a hold of him. Now he stood, half-leaning on the broken gate post to stop himself from falling flat on his face.

"Then turn around and leave." Belle glanced down at her daughter, Rosie, as the small child yanked on her hand.

"What's wrong, Mommy?" Rosie cupped her hand to her mouth and whispered loudly.

"Nothing, honey," Belle lied as she fought the urge to scoop them both up in her arms, run to the car and drive away from here and never look back. Yet there was something she couldn't explain that compelled her to stay.

"Who are they, Mom?" Her son, Jack, moved to stand next to Rosie.

"I don't know." Belle crouched down to speak to her son. "Jack, I need you to take your sister inside. Go find Grandma and tell her to take the car and leave." She slipped her car keys out of her pocket and pressed them into her son's hand.

"I'm not leaving," Jack insisted. "Grandma says I'm the man of the house and I'm supposed to protect you and Rosie."

Belle closed her eyes for a moment before inhaling deeply and opening them again. She would have a word with her mom as soon as they got out of this mess.

If they got out of it. The words hit her like a hammer on the side of the head. She was no match for the strangers in front of her. Three tall, broad-chested men and a couple of women who looked as if they knew how to handle themselves.

"Whoa!" The guy at the gate straightened and held up his hands. "No one needs to protect anyone. We're not here to cause trouble."

Belle stood up and nodded to her son. "Go find Grandma."

"Mom..." Jack's protest was cut short with a firm look from Belle and he tugged on his sister's hand, pulling her back toward the house.

"Wait. Please." The guy turned toward the others as they approached. "We just wanted information."

"Why don't you let me handle this, Rift?" One of the women hurried forward, brushing past Rift who still looked wild-eyed and half crazy. "I'm Elise."

"I don't care who you are, I want you to get back in your truck and drive away," Belle replied.

"I know you do and we're sorry to bother you, honestly." She held out her hands as she approached.

Belle kept her attention fixed on the woman while also monitoring the actions of the others who had now joined Rift at the gate. "But you *are* bothering me and even though I've asked you to leave, you are still here, *bothering* me."

She reached for her cell phone. Maybe she should call the local sheriff's office. But she didn't want to draw attention. After today, she'd hoped the specter of her uncle would disappear from their lives forever.

She'd deal with this alone.

At least she hoped she was alone. She glanced toward the house. Would her mom do as she asked and take the kids and run for safety?

"We've driven a long way to find the owner of the toy." Elise pointed to the small plush toy Rift held in his hand. "And now that we're here, we could do with your help."

"I don't know anything about the toy. It doesn't belong to either of my kids, I've never seen it before in my life." Belle jumped at a noise from inside the house.

"I've seen it before," her mom called from the window to Belle's left.

"Damn it, Mom! You were supposed to take the kids and get out of here." Belle gave her mom a reproachful look before turning back to the strangers before her.

"The toy belongs to you, Belle. It was called Jonjo or Jojo, something like that." Movement in the window told Belle her mom was coming toward the door.

Stepping to her left, Belle put herself between the door and the people in the yard. "Stay inside, Mom."

"I want to know where they got the toy from." Her mom stepped outside. "And how they knew it was yours since... I haven't seen it since your father..."

Belle swallowed hard as her mom took a deep shaking breath. "Okay, it looks as if we all need answers. So, as an act of good faith and since you are trespassing, you can go first." She waited for the strangers to answer. "Tell us where you got the toy and how you know it's mine."

Elise half-turned to look at the others. Rift sucked in a breath of the cool afternoon air and with a nod to the others, he took a faltering step forward, his chin raised as he regained his balance, and, it seemed, his wits.

"The toy has been in the possession of the police for the last forty years or so. It was among the evidence in a case of two boys who were taken from a foster home. They were found in an apartment, alone. This toy didn't belong to them, but we thought that whoever the toy did belong to might be able to give us some answers." He held out his hands. "And so here we are."

"Wait a minute." Belle put her hand up to stop him from getting any closer. "You're expecting me to believe that you managed to track me down to my dead uncle's house because of a toy that has been in police evidence for over forty years?" She gave a short laugh and shook her head. "You really should have come up with a more plausible story."

"Belle."

She closed her eyes. Belle knew that tone. "You're telling me you believe them?" she asked her mom.

Her mom stepped out of the house, an arm around Jack who still held on tightly to Rosie's hand. "I'm telling you that toy is yours." She stared at the small toy in Rift's hand. How could it be hers? None of this made sense. But she trusted her mom. "And..."

Her mom brushed her hand across her eyes and sniffed loudly. Her mom, who never cried. Her mom, who was the strongest woman, no, person, Belle had ever met.

"Mom, what is this all about?" Belle whispered.

"Your father... He..."

"He what, Mom?" Belle knew her dad wasn't one of the good guys, she'd known it since forever. Her mom refused to hide who Belle's father really was. But looking in her Mom's face now, she had hidden something. "Mom?"

"He..." She sniffed loudly and wiped the back of her hand across her nose. "I need you to know I had no idea that he... That he..."

"Your father was the man who kidnapped the two children." Rift half-turned to point at the other two men. "These are the two children." He winced. "I mean, they *were* the two children."

"I get it," Belle whispered. Only she didn't get it. Her mom told her that her dad, Murray, was a small-time petty thief who crossed the wrong people years ago and wound up dead in the street like the piece of garbage he was.

"Oh, no." Her mom covered her mouth with her hand and tightened her grip on the children.

"What do you want?" Belle stepped backward, closing the distance between her and her kids. Were they here for revenge, did they plan to take her children to get back at a man who had been dead for nearly forty years?

"We wanted to know the truth. We wanted to know if

Murray was alive." Rift nodded toward the house. "And we wanted to know about Reginald and how he fits into this."

"I'll tell you anything you want to know," Katrina replied. "But first you let my daughter and her children get in their car and drive away. You need to promise me that you won't try to follow them and that when I've answered your questions, you won't ever bother us again."

Rift's shoulders slumped forward, and the others all turned to look at him, their expressions unreadable. Yet it was a simple request. If they got their information, they'd leave and forget all about where it came from.

"My daughter wasn't out of diapers when her father died. This has nothing to do with her." Her mom stepped forward. "Take the kids, Belle." She pressed the car keys into her daughter's hand. "You go and I'll call you to come to pick me up later."

"I'm not leaving you, Mom."

"You wanted me to leave you and get the children to safety. I'm asking you to do the same thing." Her mom took a shuddering breath. "I shouldn't have asked you to come with me today. I had a sense this was going to be all messed up." Her mom put her hand to her temple. "I should have listened to myself."

"Mom." Belle held her arm around her children as she hugged her mom. "It's okay. None of this is your fault. Whatever Dad did, whatever Uncle Reggie did, none of that is on you."

"Please." Somehow Rift had made it right up to the house without them noticing. "We're not here to hurt anyone. We only want answers."

As Belle spun around and faced Rift, their eyes locked together. As she stared at the man before her, there was an undeniable attraction.

Belle sucked in a sharp breath. Katrina always said her

relationship with Murray was a mistake. Belle hadn't exactly done much better with the father of her kids who had walked out on them a couple of months ago. Was she about to make another mistake and put her trust in a man who didn't deserve it?

"Belle," her mom said gently. "It's time you knew the truth."

"The truth about what?" Belle asked.

"Your father. Your uncle." Her mom brushed her hands across her eyes and looked away, staring into the distance.

"What truth?" Belle asked. "You've always told me they weren't good people. You've never hidden the truth from me. I knew why Uncle Reggie was in prison for so long."

"I never hid the truth from you," her mom agreed. "But I never told you the whole truth. I always figured there was no need." She turned and looked at Rift, her eyes lingering on him for a long while before she added, "But I think it's time you heard it all."

"It all?" Belle placed her arms around Jack and Rosie and pulled them close, wishing they were anywhere other than here.

"There's so much you didn't know." She smiled sadly. "So much even I don't know. So much I didn't want to know."

"You're scaring me, Mom," she whispered.

When her mom finally met Belle's gaze, her breath caught in her throat.

She was right to be scared.

2

RIFT

Isn't there anything we can do to prove to our mate that we don't mean to hurt her? Rift's snow leopard asked.

I don't know if there is, Rift answered. We're strangers to her and we've brought trouble to her door.

I don't think that is her door, his snow leopard answered.

You know what I mean. She doesn't want us here. And I don't think she wants to hear what her mom has to say. Rift stepped forward and his mate instantly tensed and shot him a warning look.

"No closer." She didn't move, her arms wrapped tightly, protectively, around her children, tensed.

"Maybe we can talk while the children play?" he suggested. She looked down at them but didn't relinquish her hold. "I promise, I mean you no harm." He turned to look at the others. "None of us mean any harm."

"You might not mean me harm, but that doesn't mean you won't cause harm," she countered.

Rift bowed his head. "You're right. And I'm sorry for that."

Belle turned to look at her mom. "Does what you have to say involve these people?"

Her mom nodded. "I think it does. I also think they might be able to fill in some of the gaps for us."

Belle closed her eyes and relaxed her shoulders. "Okay, kids. Why don't you go play in the backyard for a while? But stay close to the house."

"Mom..." Jack began.

Belle hunkered down next to him and took hold of his hand. "Jack, sweetheart, I need you to watch over your sister for me. Please."

Jack stared at his mom for a long moment and then nodded briefly. "Come on, Rosie. Shall we go see if we can find the frog you saw earlier?"

"Sure." Rosie skipped away, pulling her brother after her.

"Not too far," Belle warned and looked around, scanning the area for threats.

"They're safe while we're here," Rift assured her.

"You would say that, wouldn't you?" she accused.

A small smile flickered across his lips. "I promise you, I will never hurt you. Or your children."

"He's telling the truth," her mom replied.

"And how do you know?" Belle asked. "Because as much as you trust your intuition, it's not always been great where men are concerned, has it?"

"No." Her mom's face crumpled, and she covered her mouth with her hand.

Belle rushed toward her and wrapped her arms around her, cradling her mom as she stroked her back. "I'm sorry, I didn't mean it."

"But that doesn't mean you aren't right, does it?" her mom sobbed.

Belle didn't answer. She simply held her mom in her arms. "Okay. What do you want to know?"

Caleb and Aiden approached the house with Elise and Flora by their sides. "We'd like to know about your father.

We'd like to know why he kidnapped us when we were children."

"And we also want to know if Reginald killed our parents," Aiden said and received a warning glance from Rift.

Our mate is not the enemy here. His snow leopard's tail swished from side to side as he sharpened his claws.

We need to stay calm, Rift replied. Everyone is on edge, the situation is too emotionally charged for anyone to think straight.

"Killed your parents?" Belle's face paled.

"Yes," Aiden answered tersely.

"Do you know anything about this, Mom?" Belle pulled back from her mom and held her upper arms as she studied her face. "Mom?"

"I don't know much about Reggie except what came out at the court case. We became estranged for a couple of years or more before he was arrested and sent to prison. I don't know if he killed your parents. I swear. All I know is… I would not be surprised." Katrina's mouth turned down at the corners as she fought back tears.

"And Murray?" Caleb prompted.

"I knew Murray was mixed up with some bad people. It's the main reason I took Belle and moved away." She wiped her hands across her face. "He never could hold down a decent job for more than a week. He wasn't the kind of man who would work hard eight hours a day, five days a week for an honest wage. So he earned money through dishonest means."

"He kidnapped *children*?" Belle whispered, her eyes drawn to her children as they prowled around the garden searching for wildlife.

"He... I never knew about that. Not kidnapping. I never thought him capable of that." She blew the air out of her cheeks. "Once, when he was drunk, he murmured something about children. Children who could turn into animals."

"Children who turned into animals. Did you believe him? You said he was drunk. Or was he on drugs, too?" Belle asked.

I think Belle's mom knows about shifters. But Belle doesn't. She doesn't know about shifters and so she has no idea that we are fated mates, Rift's snow leopard said.

We'll tell her when she's ready. I don't think that time is right now, Rift answered.

"No, not drugs. He was just drunk. Not even that drunk. It was during one of his ramblings. He'd sit and drink a beer while watching TV, then another beer. He used to like me to sit with him. Then he'd start to talk. He'd build himself up and tell me of all the things he was going to do to make our lives easier." Her mom gnawed on her bottom lip as she stared at Rift.

"And during one of these times, he spoke about shifters?" Caleb asked.

"Shifters?" Belle asked. "What is a shifter?"

"A shifter is a person who can change into something *else*. An animal." Her mom's eyes bored into Rift. "The police had a drawing of a man they suspected of murdering Murray. From an eyewitness. But they never found the man. I thought it was a cover-up and that he'd been killed by one of these shifters because he'd…I don't know…robbed one, assaulted one... So I searched for information on them."

"And did you find anything out? Was he killed by one of these shifters?" Belle shook her head and rolled her eyes. "Of course he wasn't because they *aren't* real."

"They're real, aren't they, Rift?" Belle's mom's eyes narrowed as she stared at him.

Katrina knows we're a shifter, his snow leopard said. I suspect she also knows about mates. And that we're Belle's mate.

That would explain why she is looking at us like that. Rift lowered his gaze and glanced at his brothers. Aiden reached out and placed his hand on Rift's shoulder and nodded, while Caleb pressed his lips together and inclined his head slightly toward Belle and a small smile of understanding crossed his brother's lips.

They know, too, his snow leopard said.

They probably knew as soon as I stumbled around like a clown and had to grab hold of the gate post to stop myself from falling flat on my face. Talk about a bad first impression.

"Rift?" Belle's anxious tone brought him back to the present.

"Shifters are real," he acknowledged. "I'm one."

"And so are we," Caleb answered, pointing at himself and Aiden.

"But not you two?" Belle asked Flora and Elise.

"No, we're fae," Flora said bluntly.

"Fae." Belle cupped her face in her hands and shook her head. "Did I make a wrong turn and end up in crazy town?"

"No, this is all true." Elise lifted her hair and revealed her pointed ears.

"You could have had plastic surgery," Belle said.

"Okay, Rift, I guess you're up." Flora clapped her hands and stepped back. "Show Belle your stuff."

"My stuff!" Rift shot Flora a confused look. "Wait, you want me to shift here? And now?"

"That would clear up this part of the discussion," Flora replied.

"You're serious?" Belle asked.

"Absolutely," Flora replied. "We've come a long way and Aiden and Caleb have waited a long time to figure out the truth about their past, and that starts with you."

"I don't have any information on what my father or Reggie had to do with you or your parents." Belle leaned to the right and fixed her gaze on Aiden and Caleb, who stood a little away from them.

"We know. But you can tell us about them. And that might lead to us uncovering the truth." Rift stepped forward. His mate stepped back.

"And proving that you are one of these shifters will help?" Belle swallowed hard as she stared at him, eyes wide.

"I don't know. But perhaps it'll help you see that you can trust me. Us." Rift met Belle's gaze, his eyes soft as he etched her face on his brain. He never wanted to forget any single thing about her. From her pale blue-gray eyes to her auburn hair, streaked with copper and tied up in a messy bun.

"You're going to show me a magic trick and that's going to make me trust you?" Belle shook her head. "I'm done with this. We have more stuff to pack up in the house. And then I'm going to take my kids home."

"Wait!" Her mom grabbed her arm and then let it go as Belle yanked it out of her grip. "Sorry. I didn't mean to grab you so hard."

"What is it, Mom? Why are you so quick to believe in all this?" Belle's eyes leveled with her mom's for a moment and they stood as if frozen in time. "You really do believe this is true."

"I don't just *believe it*," she answered. "I *know it*." She placed her hand on her heart. "I've seen shifters before." She tore her eyes from her daughter's.

"What?" Belle reached for her mom's hand and held it tight as she coaxed her to speak. "There's more. Something you're not telling me."

"Nathan is a shifter. A wolf." Her mom swallowed hard as she met her daughter's shocked expression.

"Nathan." Belle's forehead furrowed. "Nathan. *Scumbag* Nathan?"

"You shouldn't call him that. When your father died, he was very supportive."

"Was he?" Belle crossed her arms over her body. "Because

all I remember is him stealing the rent money from your purse and disappearing into the night."

"I guess he saw it as payment." There was a hard edge to Katrina's voice.

"Anyway..." Flora cut into the conversation. "Rift will shift. You'll see shifters are real and we can cut through all this pointless conversation."

I thought Flora might have grown more tactful after being around Aiden, Rift's snow leopard remarked.

She is. Most of the time. But this means a lot to her because it means a lot to her mate. Rift put his hand on Flora's shoulder as she drew closer to Belle. *We need to calm the situation.*

Then we'll shift, his snow leopard replied. *Belle will see shifters are real and we can...cut to the chase.*

Or freak her out completely and lose her forever. Rift didn't like the sound of that at all. But it was a possibility. Belle was on the defensive and seeing a man change into a snow leopard might appear like a serious threat to her children.

"This conversation might be pointless to you," Belle replied, "but this all concerns my family. My children."

Flora stared at Belle for a long moment before she replied, "*Point* taken. But you have to see that if we prove shifters are real, and your mom already knows that they are, then we can move on and not have a debate about it."

Belle closed her eyes briefly before nodding. "Go ahead. Shift." She leveled her gaze at Rift and then crossed her arms in front of her body.

"Okay." Rift sighed, this wasn't how he'd pictured his first meeting with his mate going. But he'd work with what he had. "I'll..." He looked around, pushing his senses out to check there was no one close by who might see him shift. He usually avoided shifting outside of Wishing Moon Bay and if he did shift in the world beyond, he usually waited until the cover of darkness.

"You'll what?" Belle's impatience kicked up a notch.

"I'll move around the side of the house, so the children don't see me. I don't want to scare them." He glanced at the children who were hunting around in the undergrowth. They reminded him of Penny's son, Milo. Filled with wonder and enthusiasm, they were digging in the backyard, talking quietly as if searching for something.

"Belle." Her mom touched her arm briefly. "Keep an open mind."

Belle's mouth turned down at the corners. "Mom, this isn't real."

Rift let his mind unfocus and let go of the world. He needed to get this over with and show his mate the other side of him. There was no point trying to explain anymore. Perhaps he should have told her he would never hurt her and not to scream, but he sensed Belle wasn't the screaming type.

The world faded away and his human form slipped from the world, to be replaced a few seconds later by his snow leopard, who twitched his tail as he set eyes on their mate for the first time.

Silence. No one spoke as Belle stared at the creature who had appeared as if by magic. All eyes were on her as her eyes widened and she covered her mouth with her hand. Rift didn't approach her. He sensed she needed to take the first step forward herself. He didn't want to pressure her, even though it took all his resolve to stand just out of her reach.

"Belle." Her mom touched her arm as if trying to wake her from a trance.

Belle blinked several times but didn't take her eyes off the snow leopard. "It can't be real."

"It is. Touch him." Belle's mom took her hand and led her forward. "I know it's a shock. The first time I saw Nathan shift, I thought it was an illusion, that he was playing tricks on me. But once I touched him, once I looked him in the eye, I knew he was real."

"But how?" Belle asked. "It's impossible."

"Clearly not," Flora said.

Belle turned to look at Flora, then she reached out her hand as she stepped toward the snow leopard. "You are incredible."

Rift lowered his head and closed his eyes in bliss as she ran her fingers over his head and threaded them into the soft fur along his back. He rubbed his head against her thigh and purred softly.

"Now do you believe in shifters?" her mom asked.

"It's hard to believe." Belle looked over her shoulder at her mom. "But how can I *not* believe when he's right in front of me? When I can see him and touch him?"

"I can't imagine how hard it must be to accept something that you thought impossible," Flora said gently as she approached. "When you've known about something your whole life and take it for granted, it's hard to put yourself in someone else's shoes."

Belle stroked Rift's back and then crouched down in front of him and cupped his large head in her hands. "You are the most beautiful creature I've ever seen."

Rift's snow leopard stared into her eyes and she stared right back, the connection between them flooding him with warmth. The shock of recognition on Belle's face told him she felt it, too. Would this make it easier for her to also accept that they were mates, and he was meant to be by her side for the rest of their lives?

"Okay." Flora placed her hand on Belle's shoulder and glanced toward the sound of the children who were coming closer. "It's time Rift shifted back to his human form. It's risky for him to be this exposed in your world. And we need to talk."

"In my world?" Belle twisted around to look at Flora.

"Yeah, that's something else you'll have to learn about. But maybe we should go inside?" Flora backed away, leaving Belle to stare at Rift for a few seconds longer before she let him go and rose to her feet.

Rift's snow leopard rubbed his head against her thigh once more and she tickled his head before he turned away. The air fizzed and popped as the two sides of Rift swapped places once more.

Both of them were sworn to cherish and protect their mate and her family. No matter what it took.

3

BELLE

Shifters were real. The words kept echoing around and around in her head as she stared at the man who replaced the snow leopard. Only a second ago, she'd been stroking the creature's soft fur.

She flexed her fingers. It had been real. Her senses told her the snow leopard was real. Yet her brain couldn't quite accept it. There had to be a trick. Some kind of illusion. Yet she knew that was a lie. This was the house where her uncle had spent his last months, the place was nothing special. Situated on the outskirts of a small town, there was no way Rift and his friends had set up an elaborate ruse.

Shifters were real.

"Belle." Rift ducked his head and looked up at her, searching her face for an answer to a question she didn't know.

"You're right. We should go inside." She took a shuddering breath and turned away from him.

"I'll make some coffee," her mom said and turned around, hurrying up the porch steps, her face pale.

"Jack, Rosie, we're going inside!" Belle called. "You need to come in, too."

"We'll be there in just a second," Jack replied.

"Now, please. I don't want you out here alone." Belle climbed the porch steps, aware of Rift following behind her, but the others held back, as if unsure of themselves.

"One second," Jack answered again.

"I won't ask again." Belle put her hands on her hips.

"I can keep an eye on them," Rift told her. "Well, not so much an eye, but I can use my senses. I'll know if they are close to the house and if anyone else is approaching."

"Thanks," she replied bluntly. "But we've gotten along just fine so far with normal parenting skills."

"I can see that." Rift's jaw tensed.

Belle turned to face him. "I know you probably mean well. But the last few months haven't been easy. Today was supposed to be all about closure. We came to clean out the house and hand back the keys to the landlord. We're finally putting the past behind us."

"And we arrive." Rift nodded in understanding.

"Yeah." Her eyes rested on Aiden and Caleb who were talking quietly with Elise and Flora. "You arrive."

"My brothers came looking for closure, too." He climbed another step, closing the distance between them. "We didn't come here to make trouble for you."

"I get that. I really do. But you've just shifted into a snow leopard. What am I supposed to do with that knowledge?" Belle tapped the side of her head.

A small smile played across his lips. "It's pretty awesome if you think about it."

She blew the air out of her cheeks and stared into the distance, her eyes unfocused as she pictured him fading out of the world and the snow leopard taking his place. "Yeah. It is awesome."

"What if I told you..." He chewed the inside of his cheek as he studied her, as if trying to gauge her reaction to words he hadn't said.

"There's more?" She arched an eyebrow. Maybe she didn't want to know more. Not yet. One shock at a time.

"There is." He glanced toward the cabin as the smell of fresh coffee drifted out. "But maybe that's for another time."

She stared at him for a long moment. "Another time." Although she wasn't sure she wanted there to be another time. Once they'd talked, Belle would be more than happy if this group of shifters and fae just left her life as suddenly as they'd arrived.

Belle brushed her hand down her thigh, her palm tingling as she recalled touching him for the first time, of the shock of recognition that passed between them. Did she really want him to walk out of her life and never see him again?

"Coffee is ready." Her mom was in the doorway, holding onto the doorframe as she leaned forward. "Jack, Rosie. Cookies."

"Coming!" Jack grabbed Rosie's hand and pulled her toward the house.

"Go wash your hands first," Belle instructed as they ran up the steps and clattered across the rotting wooden porch.

"Okay." They went inside the house and ran upstairs to the bathroom, casting a quick smile at their grandma.

"You spoil them," Belle told her.

"I know." Her mom winked at her. "I'm Katrina, by the way. Since we haven't been properly introduced."

"Good to meet you, Katrina. I'm Rift." Rift lifted his hand.

"I got that." Katrina nodded toward the others. "And Aiden and Caleb." She pointed at Flora. "You're Flora, but I don't think I caught your name."

"Elise." Elise mounted the porch steps and held out her hand. "It's good to meet you."

"Excuse me if I don't return the pleasantries," Katrina replied. "The jury is still out as to whether it's good to meet any of you." Her gaze rested on Rift. "But since you're here, let's go have coffee and we can talk." She turned back toward the house but then looked over her shoulder. "There are cookies for you all, too."

Rift chuckled before his expression cleared as he met Belle's gaze. She hated the effect he had on her. It was as if a part of her was no longer under her control. She held his gaze for a moment longer and then followed her mom into the house.

"The kitchen is this way." She led them past the living room where half-filled boxes held her uncle's stuff. Most of it was earmarked for the local thrift store, a couple of boxes were filled with items Katrina wanted to keep, the rest was heading for the trash.

As her eyes rested on the boxes, she couldn't help the wave of pity that swept over her. The contents of the boxes were the total sum of her uncle's life. A wasted life, one filled with a disregard for other people. Katrina often said her brother lived to hurt others.

Now, it seemed, Belle's father was also responsible for a great deal of hurt.

"Here. Sit down." Katrina swept the pile of newspapers that they'd been using to wrap anything breakable off the kitchen table and brushed her hand across the surface.

"Please, don't go to any trouble." Rift hovered close to Belle, she could sense him even when her back was turned.

"It's no trouble." Katrina was already gathering cups from the cupboards. She checked them to see if they were clean and then ran hot water into the sink and added dish soap. The whole house needed a thorough cleaning, but that wasn't their problem. Reggie had only lived here for a few short months after he'd left prison, while the dirt ingrained in the floors and the thick dust on the sideboard in the hallway had taken years to accumulate.

They were only here to collect Reggie's stuff. She glanced over her shoulder at their visitors then at her mom. On the drive here, Katrina had been anxious to get in, get Reggie's stuff, and leave as soon as possible. She'd seemed unusually nervous but with the arrival of the shifters and the fae, Katrina had forgotten her haste.

Katrina glanced up at her daughter and a soft smile slipped onto her lips before she went back to washing the cups. What did her mom know about shifters? Katrina had never said a word about them before. She'd certainly never given any indication that Nathan had been one.

A wolf shifter. Belle had often wondered if Katrina and Nathan's relationship had been more than a platonic friendship. He'd been a part of their lives for a couple years when Belle was younger. As close to a father figure as she'd ever gotten. Which didn't say much at all since Nathan treated Belle as an inconvenience more than anything else.

"I'll pour the coffee." Belle dried each cup as her mom washed them and set them down on the counter before filling them with coffee and passing them around to the group of people huddled in the kitchen.

After she'd finished washing the cups, Katrina dried her hands and then fetched a Tupperware container filled with homemade cookies she'd baked yesterday. "Help yourself."

"Thanks." Elise dipped her hand in the container and took a cookie. "Oh, these are so good."

"I like to bake," Katrina admitted. "I find it relaxing."

"They are good," Aiden agreed and eyed the remaining cookies.

"Where are the children?" Belle's heart hammered as she headed out of the kitchen and along the hallway.

"They're upstairs. I can sense them. They're running water into the sink," Rift told her.

"You can hear all that?" Belle asked. "From there." She pointed to Rift who was still in the kitchen.

"I can." He followed her to the foot of the stairs. "There's no one else around." His brows knitted together. "Who are you afraid of, Belle?"

Her breath came out in a long huff. "Who said I'm afraid of anyone?"

"I can tell by the tension in your body and the way you keep switching your attention to the front door." He stared at her, waiting for an answer.

"I don't know who I'm scared of," she said quietly, looking toward the kitchen where her mom was talking to Aiden.

"But there is someone?"

"My uncle wasn't a good man. Now he's dead..." She glanced at the boxes in the living room. "I just want to get out of here and leave the past behind. This place gives me the creeps."

"You didn't answer my question." Rift was certainly persistent.

"I don't know if there is anyone we should be afraid of. But I'm certain my mom thinks there is." Belle met his gaze. His eyes were deep pools of emotion and she wanted to dive right in and be consumed by him. Yet to let her guard down was dangerous. They had only just met and for all Belle knew, these were the people she should have been afraid of.

She tensed. If they weren't shifters, would Katrina have been more suspicious of them showing up at Reggie's house today of all days? They'd only planned on being here for three or four hours at most. What were the chances that Rift and his friends would arrive at the same time?

Rift, who admitted to having strong senses, senses that could tell him if someone was close by. What if he and the others had been waiting for Belle and Katrina to arrive? They might have been lurking around the house waiting for them to arrive. The landlord knew they were coming to clear the house. Perhaps he'd told them.

Now Katrina had invited them into the house. Anything could happen. There would be no eyewitnesses.

"What can I do to help?" Rift's offer surprised her. But what if there was something in the house that they were looking for? Perhaps Reggie had something of value that they wanted. Or evidence left over from his years of crime that they needed.

"Nothing," Belle replied. "Except drink your coffee, ask any questions you might have, and then leave and let us get on with our lives."

His eyes darkened. "If that's what you really want. But I'd rather stay by your side and protect you and your family."

"I've been doing just fine on my own. I can handle whatever comes my way," she replied with more courage than she felt. She could not let him know she was scared. And she could not let him know she suspected him and his friends of being the ones she needed to run from.

"I believe you." He pressed his lips into a thin line and fell silent for a moment before he said, "But if you had no idea about shifters, you have no idea of what other danger there might be out there."

Color flooded her cheeks. "Is that a threat?"

His shoulders sagged forward. "No. I can never hurt you."

She let out a short, humorless laugh. "Everyone is capable of hurting someone."

"I'm not capable of hurting you," he replied solemnly. "At least not intentionally."

"Why?" She rounded on him, her hands on her hips as she tilted her chin in challenge.

"Because we are mates." He pointed to her and then back

at himself as she opened her mouth to reply but no words came out. She wanted to tell him to back off, that he was crazy, but as she looked into his eyes, as she studied his expression, she didn't have the heart. He believed it. Whether it was true or not didn't matter.

Rift believed they were mates.

"And what exactly does that mean?" she asked. "To a shifter."

"Everything," he replied.

"Everything." She believed him. Hadn't she felt the connection between them? Didn't she know it to be true deep down in her soul? "Words. These are all just words and I've heard them all before."

Her temper flared, she was allowing herself to get sucked in by this man. This shifter. Well, she'd been sucked in before by a man who talked about love and loyalty and soulmates.

And he'd let her down, just as her father and Nathan had let down her mom.

"I realize I don't mean anything to you. Yet." His eyes locked with hers and he reached out to touch her arm, but then let his hand drop to his side. "But give me a chance and I will prove myself to you."

"Rift... You seem like a nice guy..." But looks could be deceptive.

"Before you say but, can I ask you to just give me a chance and keep an open mind?" He took in a shaky breath. "I'm not expecting anything from you. I'm just asking you not to push me away."

"I don't need a man in my life," she told him harshly, then pointed upstairs. "After their dad left, I promised myself I wouldn't be sucked in by a man again. My focus is on my children. You're wasting your time."

"Being there for you will never be a waste of time," he replied.

"You're determined not to do as I ask even though you said you would never hurt me." She shook her head. "I'm going upstairs to check on the children. When I come back down, my mom and I will answer your questions as best we can but then I want you to leave."

He reeled back as if she'd hit him, she'd pushed him away and it hurt her like a physical wound. Yet she wasn't going to take it back.

Even if he looked as if she'd stabbed him in the heart.

4

RIFT

She means it.

I know, Rift answered his snow leopard.

What do we do? His snow leopard paced up and down in Rift's mind before raising his head and mewling mournfully.

We give her space and try to convince her that we're here for her. Rift closed his eyes briefly and reached for the handrail as Belle ran upstairs to her children.

That sounds like a contradiction, his snow leopard said.

It is. We have to figure out how to show her she needs us without pressuring her. Belle's fiercely independent, and we have to respect that. Rift dragged his hand through his hair and went back to the kitchen.

Five pairs of eyes turned to look at him as he leaned against the counter, his arms folded across his body. Katrina passed him a cup of coffee. "You look as if you need something stronger."

"I feel as if I need something stronger," he admitted.

"She'll come around," Katrina promised. "My daughter doesn't have much trust in men, unfortunately. So you won't have it easy, but she will come around."

"What do you know about shifters?" Rift asked, his attention fixed on his mate as she went to her children.

"I know they exist, I know about the mating bond, at least I've had it explained to me." She smiled sadly, her eyes misted with tears. "Unfortunately, the person who told me about the mating bond was Nathan. He wasn't exactly trustworthy. But when I saw the way you looked at Belle, it triggered the memory I have of his explanation. I'd forgotten it, it was such a long time ago."

"Katrina has your cell phone number," Caleb spoke quietly. "If ever Belle needs you, she'll call."

"And if she doesn't need me?" Rift asked miserably.

Katrina approached him and slipped her arm around his shoulders. "I'll figure something out. Belle deserves a man who will love and cherish her. Jack and Rosie deserve a father who will love and care for them. Not the jerk who has conveniently forgotten he brought two children into this world."

"Belle's coming," Rift said quietly, and Katrina squeezed him tightly before she let him go. "Thank you."

"You're welcome." She looked toward the window. "I just hope we don't bring you trouble."

Before she could elaborate, Belle came downstairs followed by Jack and Rosie. "Grab a cookie and some soda and go eat them in the living room," Belle instructed. "Just don't mix up any of the stuff we've already packed into boxes."

"We won't," Rosie promised and took two cookies, handing one to Jack after he got two sodas from the fridge.

Belle watched the children go into the living room and then said, "Right, we still have a lot to do today so let's get the questions out of the way so you can leave."

Flora glanced at Rift, her mouth curled into a sympathetic smile. Rift nodded, his mouth twitching up at the corners. Belle might not want him here now, but with Katrina's help, there was hope.

"What can you tell us about Reggie and Murray?" Aiden asked.

"They were no good," Katrina answered.

"Can you elaborate?" Caleb asked. "Our father worked undercover and was partly responsible for Reggie's arrest and as far as we know, Reggie had our parents killed because of it. Then Murray took Caleb and me from our foster home. We can..." He cleared his throat. "We can understand why Reggie had our parents killed but we have no idea why we were kidnapped."

"Reggie was a vengeful man," Katrina began. "When he was arrested, he tried to wriggle off the hook but there was too much evidence stacked against him. Evidence, I expect, that came from your father."

"And you didn't know if he was involved in the death of our parents?" Aiden asked.

"No!" Katrina shook her head. "My brother never told me his business before I moved away. And after we left, we hardly ever spoke. It's like he thought I'd betrayed him by leaving and that suited me just fine."

"Mom wasn't involved in that world," Belle said. "She split with my father when I was very young. My dad and Reggie were friends from high school. They were very tight, isn't that right, Mom?"

Katrina nodded. "Yes." She looked down at the dirty linoleum. "I was young and stupid. Murray was a good talker. I suppose I was in awe of him and didn't see the bad in him. Not until it was too late."

"Mom had me when she was barely a teenager," Belle added.

"Reggie was five years older than me. He'd gotten into a few scrapes at school but nothing serious. At the time I started dating Murray, I had no idea of the world they belonged to. I had no idea about their criminal activities." Katrina glanced at Aiden and Caleb. "At least not at first. Then they got in deep with a gang of criminals and things escalated quickly. I saw the change in Murray. I didn't like it, but he wouldn't listen to me."

"And so Mom ended it with Murray and left." Belle went to her mom and slid her arm around her. "She took me away from my dad because she was scared."

"I moved across the country," Katrina said. "I put as much distance between me and Murray as I could. But after a few months, he persuaded me that a child needs her father. Reggie was in prison and he said he'd turned over a new leaf. And so I would drive to meet him a couple of times a month. Just so he could see Belle."

"The last time Mom was supposed to meet him, he never showed up." Belle rested her head on Katrina's shoulder. "My dad was found dead three days later."

"That was at the time he kidnapped us," Caleb said.

"I had no idea," Katrina insisted. "I genuinely believed him when he said he was going straight. He talked about getting a job."

"You had no reason not to believe him," Aiden said kindly. "None of this is on you."

"Then why do I feel responsible?" Katrina took a shuddering breath. "How could he kidnap children? And why?"

"Like my mom already told you, she has no information that can help you. She didn't know about Reggie and your parents, and she didn't know about Murray and you."

"Is there anything you can think of that might help?" Caleb asked.

"No, but it was such a long time ago." Katrina put her fingers to her temples and massaged them. "Maybe something will come back to me. But when Murray was killed and with Reggie in jail, we had a shot at a normal life. And I took it."

"You didn't visit Reggie in jail?" Caleb asked. He glanced at Aiden and then at Rift. If any of the brothers had turned out rotten if they had made mistakes and gone to prison, would the others have abandoned them?

"A couple of times at first. He told me he wanted to change and that he realized what he'd done was wrong." Katrina shook her head sadly. "But then he asked me to deliver a message to someone and I realized he was just trying to use me. When I said no, he got angry." She closed her eyes. "I can still see his face, he looked at me as if he hated me, his lips curled in a snarl. I got up and left and never went back."

"What message?" Rift asked.

"I don't know. He never told me." She put her face in her hands. "I went home, packed the apartment up, and moved. I never told him the new address and I never heard from him again."

"What about after he left prison?" Caleb asked.

"Reggie never contacted me. I didn't even know he'd been released until he died, and the authorities contacted me. I was his next of kin and it took a couple of weeks for them to trace me." She held out her hands. "That is why we are here. Closure. I can finally move on without fear of him finding us."

Belle glanced at her mom. "We should finish packing up Reggie's stuff. I want to get the kids home before bedtime."

"We can help," Elise offered. "Since we've held you up."

"No!" Belle put her hand up in protest. "We can manage."

"Why don't you at least let us help with the boxes?" Rift suggested, needing to prolong his time with his mate. He was not ready for her to walk out of his life just yet.

"We can manage," Belle insisted.

"Let them help," Katrina placed her hand on the small of her back. "It's okay to accept help from people."

"Is it?" Belle shook her head. "How many times have we told the children not to talk to strangers and here we are inviting strangers into the house and allowing them to help us?"

"This is different," Katrina insisted.

"Why?" Belle's challenge was met by a pained expression from her mom. "You're going to say because they're shifters even though Nathan was a shifter and he sure as hell wasn't trustworthy!"

"This is different because Rift is your mate." Katrina half-turned to look at Rift who moved closer. If only there was a way to prove to Belle here and now exactly what he was to her.

"Rift already told me he is my mate," Belle replied.

"And did you explain to Belle exactly what that means?" Katrina continued before Rift had a chance to answer. She turned to face her daughter. "Did he tell you that you and he are meant to be together, forever? That he didn't just show up here by chance? That it was fate because you and he are soul mates?"

"Mom." Tears misted Belle's eyes as she faced her mom. "Stop it. Those things belong in fairy tales, not real life."

"You're wrong." Flora stood up. "And your life would get a lot easier a lot faster if you don't fight it. Take it from someone who knows."

Belle glanced at Flora and Elise before she looked at Aiden and Caleb. "You are all mates?"

"We are," Elise agreed.

"And Rift is alone?" She patted her chest. "So he chose me, so he didn't feel left out."

"Belle, you can try to explain this away just because you don't want it to be real," Rift told her gently. "It's the truth."

"Whether I want it to be or not?" She raised her chin, defiance flashing in her eyes.

I think we've discovered the one way to push our mate away, his snow leopard said.

"You are my mate whether you want to be or not," Rift agreed. "But, unlike me, you have a choice. You can walk away. You can leave and never think of me again."

"And you?" Belle asked.

A sad smile flitted across his lips. He didn't want her to feel obliged to be part of his life if that wasn't what she wanted. Yet he wasn't going to lie to her either. He suspected she'd heard enough lies for one lifetime.

"You are the only woman for me. You are my mate and there's nothing I can do to change that. I've waited my whole life for you. And only you."

"That's crazy. Who would make a rule like that?" Belle asked.

"It's not a rule, it's part of who we are," Aiden chimed in.

"And you're okay with that?" Belle looked from one shifter to the others.

"It's hard, especially when you wait half your life to meet your mate." Aiden reached across the table and took Flora's hand. "But then, when you meet your mate for the first time, when you feel it in your heart." He placed his hand over his chest. "Then you understand it's worth the wait."

"I guess I'll have to take your word for it." Belle edged her way out of the kitchen at the sound of her children laughing. "I'm sorry, Rift, but this isn't something I want."

Rift nodded. He'd find a way to convince her but perhaps not today. "We should go."

Belle's eyes widened with surprise, had she been calling his bluff? "That's it?"

Rift nodded. "Yes. On one condition."

"Of course there's a condition," Belle sneered.

"I want to give you my cell phone number and if you need me, no matter what, I'll come." He locked eyes with her.

We've already given the number to Katrina, his snow leopard said.

I know, but if Belle takes it, then there's hope that she'll let us in one day. And like Aiden said, no matter how long it takes, it'll be worth the wait.

5

BELLE

That was his condition. If she took his number, he'd leave.

Belle gnawed on her bottom lip as she studied Rift. After all he'd said about mates, she was surprised he agreed to leave. She'd expected him to argue with her and make a strong case as to why she should let him stay in her life.

Was she disappointed when he agreed to leave?

"Okay." She took her phone out of her back pocket and tapped the screen. "Give me your number."

Rift reeled off his phone number and she typed it into her phone and pressed send. His phone beeped. "You sent me a text."

"Don't get excited. It's a blank text so that you'll have my number, too." She added his number to her phone book and tapped save.

"You want me to call you?" He looked confused as he stared at the small screen.

"Not really. But, since we're mates, I figured it was only fair." She slid her phone back into her pocket. "This doesn't mean I accept we're mates."

"Then what does it mean?" Flora got up from the table and came toward her. "Are you playing games?"

"No. That's not who I am." She nodded toward Rift's phone. "But if we do share this connection..." Her forehead wrinkled. She wasn't entirely sure why she'd texted him her number. Did she want him to call her?

Was that it? She kept telling him she wasn't interested when in fact she wanted him to pursue her. She wanted him to want her. She wanted to be wanted.

After Landon, the father of her children, walked out on them, she'd convinced herself she wanted to be alone. She was stronger on her own, she could be everything her children needed and more if there was no man to distract her, no man to break her heart.

Yet she loved being part of a family. Before her relationship with Landon broke down, they'd been happy. She'd been happy.

Growing up she'd always felt like the odd one out because she didn't have a father, unlike her friends. Sure, some of them might be from split families, but their dads were still around, still part of their lives.

But Murray was gone. Dead.

She hated that her children didn't have a dad who was part of their lives. Landon might not be dead, but he might as well be. He'd only seen them a handful of times since he'd left. It was as if he'd forgotten about them. He'd moved on and found a new woman. A woman who had children of her own, children he'd become a father to.

If Belle believed what Rift said about mates, her children could have a father again, they could be a family again.

But Nathan had promised her mom he'd look after her and be part of her life. Nathan, who had no time for Belle. He'd only been interested in Katrina, taking advantage of her at every opportunity, aware of how much she craved his attention. Nathan, who had treated Belle as an inconvenience.

Nathan, who was a shifter.

If she let Rift into their lives, would he treat Jack and Rosie the same way Nathan had treated Belle?

She wasn't taking that chance. No way. Even if Rift said they were mates.

"You feel it," Flora stated. "But you're afraid. Afraid to give in to it."

"I'm not afraid," Belle replied but who was she kidding? Perhaps she was afraid of giving her heart, giving her love, to someone more than she was afraid of anything else. More than she was afraid that Katrina was right and there might be people from Reggie's past who might be lurking in the shadows.

"Then give Rift a chance," her mom said.

"Mom," she warned.

"What? Do you think I like seeing you alone? You have so much love to give, and you deserve the love of a shifter." Her mom covered her mouth with her hands and sucked in a sobbing breath. "This is all my fault."

"What is your fault?" Belle asked, her frustration growing.

"After everything that happened between me and your father and then Nathan, and you and Landon, you're afraid to open your heart and let someone else in." Katrina's expression showed the guilt she shouldered.

"Mom, can we let this go?" She closed her eyes for a second, it was as if they were all ganging up on her trying to pressure her into something she'd already told them she didn't want.

"Belle is right." Rift beckoned to the others. "We should go. You need to finish up here and, unless you need our help, we're just getting in the way."

He nodded at his friends, his jaw tense as he cast a

lingering glance in Belle's direction. So that was it, he was going to leave. Or perhaps he was playing hard to get. He probably figured she'd stop him before he left the house. Well, he was wrong. Whatever she felt for him wasn't real. It couldn't be real, they'd only just met.

There wasn't much Belle believed in and love at first sight would never make it onto the shortlist.

Belle headed for the front door and pulled it open. She scanned the backyard checking, as she had from the moment they arrived here, that there was no one lurking close by. There was no one. As she turned around, she was met by Rift's unfocused stare. He was scanning the area, too, only his senses went much farther than hers.

As Elise walked past, she grabbed Belle's hand. "I know this doesn't seem real, it doesn't seem possible, but you saw Rift shift. Is it too much of a reach to believe that mates are real, too?"

Belle didn't pull away as she took a deep breath. She could sense Rift, it was as if she could feel his body heat radiating out and surrounding her. "It's not that I don't believe it," she replied. "But I need to focus on my children. I don't need any distractions. I don't want to be torn between them and a man."

"That's never going to happen," Elise answered. "Rift loves children. He would love and care for your children like they were his own."

"I don't want to take that risk," Belle answered and pulled her hand out of Elise's.

"Elise, it's okay." Rift touched the fae on the arm and she moved away, the others following as they headed for their truck.

Rift hesitated and didn't follow directly behind her. Instead, he lingered on the porch, his eyes downcast as he shuffled his feet. Belle looked away, staring at the neighboring house, not wanting to witness the pain in his eyes.

"I'll call you," she finally said.

Rift's head jerked up and he searched her face. He was trying to figure out if she meant it. "No pressure. I promise."

She nodded. "I just need time to get my head around all of this." She waved her hand at him but also encompassed Reggie's house. "It's been a rough few months. I hoped once we'd cleaned out the house that things would settle down. You know, go back to how they were before."

"I can understand that," Rift replied.

She nodded absently. "Then you show up and the more I'm around you..." She placed her hand on her heart. "The more a part of me says that this is how it's supposed to be. Me and you."

"And that's scary." He sighed, his eyes fixed on hers. "I'm here for you *and* the children. Whatever you need. Just ask."

"That's what scares me," she blurted out her admission. "The children are my priority, and they always will be. I don't want to be pulled in two directions. Not when they need me so much."

"I want to be part of their lives as much as I want to be a part of yours," he assured her.

"Then, I'll call." She crossed her arms over her body and took a step back toward the house.

Rift watched her for one long moment before he turned away and headed for the truck. He passed through the broken gateway where less than an hour ago he'd stood, holding onto it for support.

Did she do that to him? Had she literally made him go weak at the knees?

Belle watched as he reached the truck and got inside. She didn't move as he opened the door, took one last lingering look at her, and then climbed into the passenger seat.

Only when the truck drove around the side of the house and disappeared from view did she move. Her steps short, unsure, as if she were walking away from the best thing that could ever happen to her.

Yet the best thing that ever happened to her was inside the house. Jack and Rosie were giggling, their voices high with excitement.

"What are you two up to?" Belle hurried inside. She wanted to get the rest of the stuff packed away so they could leave within the hour. Rift had assured her there was no one around, but the hairs on the back of her neck said otherwise.

"Rosie is being a princess," Jack told his mom as she entered the living room. "I said I'd make her a castle out of the boxes."

"We don't have time for that." Belle closed her eyes, she never usually snapped at the children. But the events of the day were wearing on her nerves.

Jack moved to Rosie's side and slipped his arm protectively around her shoulder. "We were just playing."

"I'm sorry. I just want to get home." Belle crouched down and held out her hands. "I love you guys. I'm sorry I snapped."

Rosie pulled on Jack's hand, after a moment's hesitation, he followed his sister into a group hug. "We love you, too, Mommy."

"It's gone quiet in here." Katrina entered the living room and went to a half-empty box. "Is everything all right?"

"We are just about to start packing the boxes." She glanced up at her mom. "Not that there's a lot left."

"Not much at all. No keepsakes, no photos." Katrina sorted through a small stack of books, most of which she put in the box marked 'thrift store.' "I don't think these were even his. Reggie was never a big reader."

"Let's just get rid of it all." Belle shuffled over to her mom under the watchful gaze of Rosie.

"Good idea." Katrina piled all the books into a box and then closed the flaps, her hands smoothing over the cardboard in a steady rhythm as if she were stroking it.

"Mom?" Belle put her hand on her mom's shoulder. "If you'd rather keep some of it..."

"No. It just makes me sad, that's all." Katrina pressed her lips together as her bottom lip trembled.

"I'll start putting the boxes in the trunk. The landlord will be here in an hour. I want to be on the road as soon as he's gone." Belle picked up one of the boxes and carried it out to the car. "Kids, if there's anything you can carry, bring it out."

"Okay," Jack replied from the kitchen, where he and Rosie had gone. They were talking quietly together, Belle suspected they were secretly eating more cookies, but she let it slide.

It had been a long day already and they had a long drive ahead of them. She'd planned to drop Reggie's stuff off at the local thrift store, but since there wasn't much, she'd take it all home and then get rid of it all.

That way they could go through it all one more time to check if there was anything of value or anything sentimental her mom might want.

An hour later, they were in the car driving away from the house. The landlord had gotten his keys back, although he'd argued he'd expected the house to be cleaned, too. Katrina had proceeded to give him a tour of the house, pointing out that there was no way that amount of dirt had accumulated in the last couple of months.

When she'd questioned the amount of rent Reggie had paid and mentioned how the state of the house might have contributed to his poor health, the landlord had made a hasty exit.

As she drove away from the house, she took one last look

at the ramshackle building with some relief. Her mom was finally free of her brother who had caused her nothing but heartache.

Their future lay ahead.

Did that future include a certain snow leopard shifter?

6

RIFT

"How are you feeling?" Caleb turned to Rift who was staring out of the window as they drove away from his mate.

"How do you think?" Rift didn't look at his brother, he didn't want to talk.

"I'd feel as if I'd been kicked in the gut and then had my insides ripped out," Caleb answered.

"Is that helpful?" Elise asked her mate.

"I'm trying to show Rift that I empathize with him." Caleb leaned forward, he was seated on the other side of the passenger seat with Elise sandwiched between them. "But I believe things will find a way of working out."

"I agree," Aiden said from the driver's seat. "You and Belle are meant to be together. You've seen the same thing happen with four of your brothers. Do you think you're that special? It won't work out for you?"

Rift turned from the window and chuckled. "Well, if you put it like that."

"He's right," Elise punched him lightly on the arm. "You aren't anything special."

"Ouch!" He rubbed his arm even though it didn't hurt.

"I was helping take your mind off things," Elise answered.

"I know what else might take your mind off things." Aiden looked at Rift in the rearview mirror. "Food."

"Ah, my bear shifter brother, always thinking of his stomach." Rift leaned forward and patted Aiden on the shoulder. "You're right, though. It's been a long drive and we should stop for food."

Rift's snow leopard flicked his tail as he paced around in his head. He was agitated, his pent-up energy needed an outlet. If not, Rift thought his head would explode.

Eat quickly and then let's go for a run, his snow leopard suggested and flexed his claws.

That's a good idea, Rift agreed. As long as we find somewhere to eat close by. They were driving along the edge of a mountain range, with thick forests covering the lower slopes. We don't exactly blend in if we stop in a town.

I could pretend I'm an oversized cat, his snow leopard insisted.

Rift didn't even bother to reply, they both knew that wasn't true. Even in the mountains, he didn't exactly blend in. But the trees and undergrowth made it easier for him to hide.

"There's a truck stop ahead." Aiden slowed the vehicle. "Shall we eat here?"

"As long as the place is clean and it has a restroom then I'm okay with it," Flora said.

"Agreed," Elise added. "I could do with a nice cold drink and something warm to eat."

"Are you turning into a bear shifter, too?" Rift joked.

"I will never have that kind of an appetite," Elise replied.

"Hey, I don't eat that much," Caleb insisted.

"You do," Elise told her mate. "I sure hope when we have children that they don't eat as much as you. I don't know how Valerie kept you all fed when you were growing up."

"We were always raiding the kitchen," Aiden admitted. "Valerie used to threaten that she'd put a padlock on the fridge to keep us out."

Rift chuckled at the memories before his expression faltered. He pictured Jack and Rosie, they looked like good kids and Belle obviously loved them a huge amount. What he wouldn't give to be their father. What he wouldn't give to have children of his own.

Would that ever happen now?

If Belle doesn't call, what are we going to do? His snow leopard sat down and licked his large paws.

I don't know, Rift admitted. But Aiden is right, we're nothing special, there's no way fate would have decided that we would find our mate only for us to never see her again. There has to be a way. We just haven't thought of it yet.

Then get thinking, his snow leopard told him. I don't want to live another hour without seeing her, let alone a day, a month, or a year.

Rift opened the truck door as Aiden parked in front of the truck stop. We'll need to be patient. We can't make her want us in her life. We need Belle to make up her mind to let us in.

I suppose you're right, but I don't like it, his snow leopard grumbled.

So you keep saying. Rift held the door open, and Elise slid across the seat and got out.

"The air is so clear." Elise turned around, her chin tilted up as she took in the dense pine forest surrounding them. "I can smell the sun on the pine trees."

"I think I might go for a run." Rift's appetite was never as big as his bear shifter brothers', but after meeting and losing his mate within the space of an hour, it had completely disappeared.

"Do you want one of us to come with you?" Caleb slipped

his arm around his mate's neck, reminding Rift of what he'd lost.

"No, you go eat. I'd like some time on my own to think. Maybe you could grab me something to go?" He backed away from the others.

"Sure." Caleb placed his hand on Rift's shoulder. "We'll work it out. You're not alone in this."

Yet as Rift nodded and backed away, he felt very much alone. How could his brothers know what he was going through when they had their mates by their sides?

"Thanks, Caleb." He took a shuddering sigh. "Thank you all. I'm grateful to have such a wonderful family to support me."

"We're all here for you." Aiden grabbed him and pulled him into a bear hug. "Just don't shut us out."

"I won't." Rift glanced toward the cool shade of the pine forest surrounding them. "I just need to run and clear my head."

"Go." Aiden patted his chest as he let his brother go. "We'll be waiting for you."

"Just don't be too long," Flora called.

"I told Valerie we'd be back in Wishing Moon Bay before dark," Aiden added.

"I'll be back before you've finished eating," he promised.

They watched him as he jogged down the road, and then crossed into the forest on the opposite side. He could feel their eyes on his back. Full of sympathy, full of understanding. His breath caught in his throat and he swallowed down a sob.

This should be the happiest day of our lives. His snow leopard itched to break free and run like a shadow through the forest.

It still is the happiest day, Rift replied even though happy wasn't what he felt at all. We met our mate, at least we no longer have to search for her.

Yes, we met her, but we don't exactly know where she is. She gave us her cell phone number but where does she live? How will we find her? His other side snarled in anguish. If she doesn't want us to find her, we might never see her again.

We must believe in fate. We must trust in fate. With that, Rift let go of the world around him and disappeared, to be replaced a couple of seconds later by a stunning snow leopard who leaped forward, running through the undergrowth, with twigs and branches snagging at his fur.

The creature ran on. His stride lengthened as his muscles bunched as he climbed uphill, running as if his very life depended on it.

Using his shifter senses, he weaved in and out of the trees, always keeping a fix on the location of the truck stop. He didn't want to get lost in this strange wilderness. The others didn't need the worry about searching the mountain for him.

On and on he ran, his heart pumping blood through his veins as he strained to climb a steep section of the forest. All around him, life carried on as his snow leopard's stealth kept him hidden from the creatures that lived in the forest.

Birds called to their mates, small mammals searched for food to take home to their offspring, while Rift's snow leopard ran on alone, aware of the long, lonely life that stretched ahead of him if he didn't figure something out.

Perhaps he could ask Oscar to track Belle down. Then he could visit the town where she lived and arrange to accidentally bump into her.

His snow leopard chuffed and shook his head. That's the worst idea I've ever heard. Belle's a smart woman, she'd see right through any trick like that. We'll need to be smart if we don't want to appear like a stalker.

Rift let go of the image of himself walking along the street as Belle and her children were coming toward him. He let go of the image of their eyes meeting and a small smile curving her lips. But he could not let go of the image of her beautiful face, worry lines creasing her mouth and the haunted look in her eyes.

Yet when he'd left her as they'd driven away from the house, everything had seemed fine. They were packing the last of Reggie's things away and then they would leave, go back to their old life.

Without him.

Yet a nagging doubt in the back of his mind warned him all was not right. Was there something she hadn't told him?

Why would she tell us anything? His snow leopard leaped over a thick fallen tree trunk. She doesn't know us. She certainly doesn't trust us. It was there in her eyes.

Maybe she just doesn't trust men, Rift mused. Her father and uncle were bad men, and the father of her children has walked out on them.

His snow leopard snarled. What if that's what's keeping us apart?

Rift's heart hammered in his chest. I never thought about that at the time. Belle might want the father of her children back even though he's hurt them and let them down. She might still be in love with him. Surely fate wouldn't be that cruel.

And yet we believe that fate is cruel enough to show us our mate and then let her walk out of our lives.

Rift's mood lightened. Which means we will find a way back to her. We will find a way to make her part of our lives. One day, she'll wear our ring on her finger.

She will. His snow leopard's energy levels shot up and he flattened out, running fast, covering the ground at a sprint until they broke out of the forest and into the open mountainside.

There the snow leopard stopped. He lifted his head and

scented the air. Rain was coming. It was time to turn around and run back to the others. It was time to eat. Time to prepare.

When they got back to Wishing Moon Bay, he'd look for a bigger place to live. When Belle came back into his life, he wanted to be ready to make a home with her.

What if that home is not in Wishing Moon Bay? His snow leopard had a point.

Our home is where she is, Rift said, and yet he couldn't help but feel a twinge of disappointment.

He'd move wherever his mate wanted to be. It made sense that she wouldn't want to leave her life behind. The children would have school and friends, they wouldn't want to be uprooted to live in a strange town.

Yet there was a twinge of regret, a longing to raise his family in the town he knew so well. He'd dreamed of showing his children the wonders of the town, he longed to teach them about the people who lived there, the shifters, the witches and the warlocks, the fae.

He wanted his children to grow up alongside his brother's children.

Let go of the future, his snow leopard told him bluntly. Look at the world around us. Look at its beauty. Wherever we are, wherever we live, we will find that beauty. And if we must live elsewhere, we can always visit Wishing Moon Bay on weekends and vacations. It will always be our home.

Rift nodded. It's just a place. Our family will still be our family.

And we'd have a mate.

If she called.

7

BELLE

"I'm sorry. I know that ever since Reggie's death, it's like there's been a black cloud hanging over us." Katrina stared straight ahead, she'd been in her own world ever since they left the house.

"It's not your fault, Mom. We don't get to pick our family, do we?" Belle patted her mom's hand.

"No, we don't." Katrina turned to her daughter. "Will you promise me one thing?"

Belle sighed. "Does this promise involve a certain snow leopard shifter?"

"It does." Katrina straightened up and grasped Belle's hand. "You *are* his mate."

"So he said."

"But I don't think you were listening. I don't think you understood what he meant. You and Rift are meant to be together. That's how shifters work. They have this bond, and they know who their mate is. They know deep down in their soul who they are meant to spend the rest of their lives with." Katrina looked at Belle with tears in her eyes.

"Did Nathan tell you he was your mate?" Belle winced at her mom's pained expression. "I'm sorry."

"No, you have a right to ask..." She took a shuddering breath. "No. He didn't."

"I'm sorry." Belle glanced at her mom. "I didn't mean what I said back at the house. I know Nathan hurt you."

"You were right, though. I have a terrible taste in men." She rubbed the backs of her hands across her eyes. "But it is different for you and Rift."

"How do you know so much about shifters?" Belle glanced in the rearview mirror, she didn't want the children to hear them talking about Rift shifting into a snow leopard. Thankfully, they were both engrossed, Jack was playing a game on his phone and Rosie was reading a book about princesses. Belle smiled softly, she loved her kids so much. She'd do anything for them. They were her life.

"Like I told you, after what your father said and then after he died, I did some research. I found a bar where shifters drink and that's where I met Nathan." She inhaled deeply and looked down at her hands.

"Did you love him? I mean really love him?" Belle asked.

"Nathan?" Her head jerked up.

"No. My dad. I know you left him but that doesn't mean that you didn't love him. We've never really talked about it." Belle glanced in the rearview mirror and took a left turn. The road snaked along the side of the mountain, weaving through dense forest before they joined the highway on the other side.

"I loved him. At the time I was completely smitten. He was larger than life and he treated me well. At least at first. Then he slowly eroded my self-confidence. He'd ask me if I put on weight. He told me my clothes didn't suit me or that my friends had been talking about me behind my back. He..."

Tears trickled down her cheeks and she sniffed loudly and searched her purse for a tissue.

"I'm sorry. I shouldn't have asked." Belle chewed the inside of her cheek as she fought to control her emotions. She'd never know Murray. She'd always wondered what her life would have been like if her mom hadn't left him. Would he still be alive? Would he have taken a different path?

As she side-eyed her mom, she was grateful he hadn't been a part of their lives. Katrina was the best mom she could ever have hoped for. Kind, caring, and supportive. Things would have been so different if Murray had been a part of their lives.

"No, it's good that you know about him. He is part of you." She glanced out of the window. "Am I a terrible person?"

"Mom." Belle reached for her mom's hand. "Why would you say that?"

"Because..." She lowered her head and covered her face with her hand. "Because the day I learned he was dead, I felt relief." She let out a long, shaky breath.

"You were free." Belle squeezed her mom's hand. "I think anyone would have felt the same way."

"I mourned for him. I mourned for you. I think...I hoped that your father would one day change and realize what he was missing out on. When Reggie went to prison, I thought that might be the catalyst that brought us back together. But instead..." Katrina blew her nose hard. "Look at me crying over something that happened so long ago."

"Memories live on through us," Belle told her. "And Reggie dying has brought them all to the surface. But now that the house is cleaned out, we can move on again."

"Can we?" Katrina's eyes slid sideways, and she looked at Rosie's reflection in the side mirror.

"Yes." Belle's jaw tightened.

"Sometimes the ghosts of the past haunt us no matter what we do."

"I don't believe in ghosts." Belle fixed her eyes on the road. There was no point trying to figure it out now. She pressed her fingers to her temple, a slow dull thud brought the threat of a headache and she wanted to get them all home before it became too bad.

She glanced in the rearview mirror once more. She couldn't ignore the twinge of apprehension when she noted the same vehicle had been following them for the last few miles. It had been behind them when they turned onto the mountain road and it was still there.

Belle closed her eyes briefly and took a deep breath. She was seeing monsters where there were none. This road was well used, it cut across the country, taking a good half an hour off the alternative route that went around the mountains.

"Are you okay?" Katrina picked up on her unease.

"Yeah." Belle rubbed her temple again. "I have a headache coming on."

"It's been a stressful day." She leaned closer. "It's not every day you meet the man you're supposed to spend the rest of your life with."

"Mom," she hissed and checked to see if either of the kids were listening. Thankfully, they weren't.

However, as she switched her gaze to check on the vehicle behind them, she noted it was slowly closing the distance between them.

Belle inched her foot down on the accelerator, not enough to be noticeable but enough to maintain the distance between them and the vehicle behind.

However, the other vehicle kept closing in on them. Belle rolled her shoulders, trying to keep calm. She needed to think clearly. Was there any other road they could turn off and head toward a town? Anywhere where there were other people. If someone were after them, the best thing they could do was stay in plain sight of lots of people.

She mentally pulled up the map. As far as she could recall, there were no towns until they got to the other side of the mountain. Sure, there were houses dotted along the route, but it was risky to try to get help there.

Belle also didn't like the idea of taking trouble to a stranger's door.

Focusing on the road, Belle eased her foot down farther on the accelerator. The road wasn't wide enough for the other car to pass so as long as she kept going, they should be safe.

If there wasn't anything, or anyone, in front of them. What if this were an ambush and as she rounded a bend, she'd find an obstruction that might send them crashing off the road?

Cold sweat prickled along her spine as her mind raced around in circles, trying to figure out a solution. Had Rift and the others been part of something bigger? Something more sinister?

She let out a long breath. She was overreacting. Why would anyone want to ambush them? The guy behind was in a hurry, that was all. She should just pull over and let him pass.

"Belle." Katrina looked over her shoulder. "What's wrong? And don't say nothing."

"I think the car behind us is following us. But I'm overreacting." She checked the mirror again. The vehicle, a truck, was so close she could see the faces of the occupants.

Katrina glanced in the side mirror. "They're pretty close."

"When the road widens, I'll pull over so they can pass." She checked the rearview mirror again.

"What if they're trying to get in front so they can make us

stop?" Katrina turned around in her seat and stared out of the back window.

"Why would they?" Belle wasn't the only paranoid person in the car.

"I don't know." Katrina turned back around and clasped her hands together in her lap, but her eyes kept drifting toward the side mirror.

"Mom?" Belle glanced at her mom's pale face.

Katrina didn't answer.

"Why would you think anyone would try to make us stop? I don't think they're trying to carjack us. This thing is far too old to be worth the trouble." Belle tried to lighten the mood, but it didn't work.

"A couple of weeks after Reggie left prison, I got a visit. They said they were from the authorities, that Reggie hadn't attended some meeting or other. I told them I hadn't seen or heard from Reggie since he left prison."

"I thought you didn't know Reggie had left prison?" Belle flexed her hands on the steering wheel, her palms were sweating. This had been a day for shocking news, and it wasn't over yet.

"I didn't want you to worry about it, not when you were dealing with Landon leaving." Katrina glanced at the children on the backseat, but they weren't listening. "It just didn't seem important since Reggie hadn't bothered to contact us."

"Okay, anything else you'd like to share?" Belle glanced in the rearview mirror once more, her fear growing.

"No, they left and that was it." Katrina shrugged.

"But now you think it's something to do with the guys in the truck behind us?" Belle's heart hammered as she forced herself to stay calm and focus on the road ahead.

"I think..." She turned in her seat and stared out of the back window once more. "I think one of the guys who came to the house is in the front of the truck."

"What?" She gripped the wheel tighter as panic filled her. "Are you sure?"

"No." The lines around Katrina's mouth deepened. "But..."

"Okay, we'll just keep on driving. Like nothing is wrong." Belle blew out a slow breath, fighting her rising panic as she checked on her children in the back seat.

The truck was closer now. Too close.

Her car would be no match for the truck's bull bars if they tried to run her off the road.

She swallowed hard. If the truck rammed into the back of her car at the right speed and angle, she'd lose control and likely smash into a tree, or worse, go over the edge of the road and roll down the mountainside.

"What can they want?" Katrina asked. "I didn't have any contact with Reggie for years."

"I don't honestly know, Mom. But they've been following us for a while. What better place to ambush us than here where no one will see?" Belle prayed someone else would come by. Perhaps they would catch up with another car. She unconsciously pressed her foot down harder on the accelerator, the whites of her knuckles showing as she gripped the wheel.

"Careful." Katrina pressed her lips together. "If we go too fast, there's a chance we'll take a curve wrong and crash." She glanced at the dashboard. "You need to slow down."

"Mom." Belle glanced at her mom for a second as they traveled along a relatively straight part of the road.

The driver of the truck made his move. The engine revved and the truck shot forward, heading for the side of the car. There might be enough room to pass if Belle moved over to the side of the road and slowed down.

"Don't let them pass." Katrina gripped the edges of her seat.

"The car is no match for their truck." Belle looked in the

side mirror. The truck was almost level with the trunk of the car. She had to make a decision.

"You're right. If they don't pass and they smash into the car, we're in trouble," Katrina's voice rose in panic.

"Mommy?" Rosie's voice wavered as she dropped her book.

"Sit still," Belle commanded. "Just hold on tight. There's a crazy driver behind us."

"They're coming up the side," Rosie wailed as the hood of the truck drew level with her window. There was no way to outrun them. She needed a new plan.

Up ahead there was a trail mouth that opened up on the side of the road and led into the trees. If she slowed down, she could pull off the road and let them pass. A quick glance told her the truck was still coming, edging farther alongside them.

Belle eased her foot off the accelerator and then pressed down on the brake, guiding the car into the trail mouth.

The truck sped past them, giving Belle a quick chance to look at the people inside. The guy closest to the window stared at her, his eyes fixed on her face before he turned away.

Her heart hammered in her chest as she stopped the car, her fingers clutching the steering wheel so tightly she had to flex them a couple of times before she loosened her grip.

"They're slowing down," Katrina whispered.

Belle raised her head, the truck's red brake lights were bright under the dark canopy of trees. "Hold on tight."

She pulled forward across the road, and then put the car in reverse. As she pulled back into the trail mouth, the truck driver began backing down the road.

"Hurry." Katrina gripped the door as Belle swung the car around. She pulled forward again, there was no way she'd make it in one go without risking the wheel going off the edge of the road.

She reversed again, aware of the approaching truck speeding toward them.

The wheels spun as she drove forward, the wheel turned hard as she finally made it back around and headed back the way they'd come.

"Mommy, what's happening?" Rosie wailed as she swung right and left in her seat.

"We're going back the way we came," Belle replied.

"Why?" Rosie put her hand out to catch her book as it slid off her lap.

Damn it! What the hell did they want? The boxes in the trunk? There must be something in Reggie's stuff that they wanted. But what? It all looked like junk, aside from the books.

Perhaps there was something hidden in them?

She glanced in the rearview mirror. They were trying to turn the truck around, but the vehicle was too long, and they seemed to have gotten themselves wedged across the road. She pressed her foot down on the accelerator and drove like the devil himself was on their heels.

"What are we going to do?" Katrina asked.

"Call the police," Jack suggested.

"Good idea." Belle glanced at her mom. "Call them."

"And say what? What are the chances they'll find us before..." She closed her mouth, her jaw tense.

"They'll find us."

"And then what? Those guys will go to the ground and we'll go home..."

Her mom's words brought up all kinds of horrifying scenarios in her mind. "They know where you live."

"They do."

"Then what do you suggest?" Belle asked. "We can't run forever."

"We should call Rift."

Belle swung her head around to face her mom. "I am not dragging him into this. Whatever this is."

"I don't think you have a choice," Katrina replied.

Belle raised her eyes, glimpsing the truck in the rearview mirror before the road curved to the right and they disappeared from view. Her mom was right, they were out of choices.

But if they called him, would he come?

There was only one way to find out.

8

RIFT

Rift ran through the pine forest, he could hear a car in the distance, signaling he was close to the road. Slowing his pace, he waited until he could see the road before he slipped behind a thick shrubby bush and shifted back into his human form.

Stretching his arms above his head, he leaned from side to side, trying to get rid of the kinks in his body from being in the truck for too long. He couldn't wait to get back to Wishing Moon Bay, but he hated the idea of going home without his mate.

He looked up at the sky, it was an hour or two past noon and if they wanted to get back before dark, they needed to get back on the road soon.

His stomach rumbled. First, he needed to eat. He jogged down to the road, crossed over in the same place as before, and hurried on to the truck stop. The aroma of steak and fries met him as he opened the door and went inside.

"There you are." Aiden was at the counter talking to the cashier. Next to him was a cardboard container. "I was worried your food would get cold." He nodded toward the packet of food.

"And I was worried we'd be hanging around here for hours." Flora picked up the food and handed it to him. "I persuaded Aiden to let you eat this in the truck as long as you promise not to wipe your greasy fingers on his upholstery."

Rift cracked a smile. "You're so kind and thoughtful."

"Don't get used to it." Flora stared at him for a long moment as he sniffed the food. "You look a little better. The run did you good?"

"It did. I've cleared my head." He backed toward the door as Aiden finished paying and slipped his wallet into his pocket. "If I also fill my stomach, I should be feeling halfway to normal."

"I'm sorry about what happened with Belle," Flora told him as Caleb and Elise left the table they'd been seated at and came to join them. "But I am certain it'll work out."

"It has to." Elise screwed up her mouth. "You deserve to be happy, Rift." She linked arms with him, and they went outside. "We just have to figure out how to make Belle see that she needs you in her life."

"That might be a little difficult if I'm in Wishing Moon Bay and she is..." He looked up at the thick pine forest. "Wherever she is."

"It'll work out." Elise let go of his arm and he unwrapped the food. It looked good and the smell assailed his senses.

"I hope so." Rift was done talking about it for now. As much as he appreciated their concern, he didn't want to spend the entire drive home going over and over the subject. There was nothing more he could do, nothing more he could say.

Unless he tracked Belle down like a stalker, he'd have to trust in fate to bring them back together.

Just as fate brought us together in the first place, his snow leopard reminded him.

Exactly like that, Rift agreed.

They all got in the truck and Rift started on his food, the fries were golden and delicious while the steak was cooked to perfection. He relished the flavors as they drove on, and he ignored the nagging voice in his head telling him they were getting farther and farther away from his mate.

"Thanks for the food, Aiden." Rift wiped his fingers on a napkin.

"You're welcome. I wish there was more I could do for you." Aiden glanced in the rearview mirror and offered a sad smile.

"I know. And I appreciate it, I really do. But I suppose I just have to move on and hope that things turn out the way they're supposed to." Rift wiped the back of his hand over his eyes. He was tired, emotionally drained and now that he'd eaten, he just wanted to curl up under his bedcovers and go to sleep. But they were still a long way from home.

As he stared out of the window, the steady thrum of the engine lulled him to sleep, his eyes growing heavier as the wheels turned.

"Rift." Elise dug him in the ribs, and he jumped, forcing his heavy eyelids open as he reached for his phone.

"I must have dozed off." He tapped the screen, his eyes unfocused for a second before they widened, and he was suddenly wide awake. "It's Belle."

"Belle is calling you?" Caleb leaned forward and stared at his brother.

"Yeah." Rift locked eyes with his brother as confusion filled him.

"Well, answer it," Flora ordered.

"I am." He tapped the screen again. "Hello, Belle?"

"Katrina." Belle's mom sounded breathless as if she'd been running.

"Is everything all right?" Rift was instantly focused as he waited for the reply.

"No." Katrina gasped.

"What's wrong?" He tapped Aiden on the shoulder and his brother pulled over to the side of the road.

"We're being chased. There's a truck following us and..." Katrina hiccupped as she stifled a sob.

"Where are you?" Rift demanded.

"On a mountain road." Her voice was muffled for a moment and he could hear Belle's voice in the background. "When we left the house, we took a mountain road that headed toward the highway."

"I have the map on my phone." Elise tapped her phone screen and presented it to Rift. "Here's the house where we met. I think this might be the road they're on." Elise leaned forward and traced her finger along a road that followed the edge of the mountain range.

"Okay, I think we know which road you're on." Rift pointed to Aiden and Elise flipped the phone around and showed the bear shifter the route they needed to take.

"Hurry." Fear laced Katrina's voice.

"We will." Rift leaned to the right as Aiden swung the truck around and headed back in the direction they'd come from. "Can you stay on the line?"

"I'll try." Katrina gasped as tires squealed. "Careful, Belle."

"I'm trying," came Belle's muffled reply.

"What's happening?" Rift asked. "Can you tell me how close they are to you?"

Katrina was quiet for a moment. Then she answered, "We can't see them right now, the road is too winding."

"Good, try to keep ahead of them. We'll meet you soon." He sounded more confident than he felt.

"Maybe we should turn off the road and hide in the trees," Katrina suggested. "There are a couple of trails."

"No!" Rift snapped before calming his voice. "If they are shifters, they'll be able to sense you. You'll just end up trapped with no way out."

"I forgot shifters can sense people even if they aren't their mate," Katrina replied.

"They'll be able to sense you for some distance. I'd expect you to need at least a couple of miles or more between you and them to lose them completely." He glanced at Caleb. "That gives me an idea."

"Any idea of how we're going to get out of this is fine by me," Katrina replied.

"Okay, we'll be turning onto the road in about half a mile." Rift glanced at Aiden, his brother's face was set firm, his focus completely on the task of reaching Belle and her family before they came to harm.

"We're about a mile away from the end of the road." Katrina let out a small cry.

"Are you still okay?" Rift asked.

"We're good," she replied, although she didn't sound good.

Rift's snow leopard snarled, he wanted to spring free of the truck and run across the mountainside to his mate. As the distance between them lessened, he could sense her. *Our mate.*

We'll get to them, don't worry, Rift assured his snow leopard.

"Do you want to fill us all in on your plan?" Aiden glanced at Rift in the rearview mirror.

"We're going to trade passengers," Rift replied.

"Trade passengers?" Elise was surprised by the plan.

"Yes." He spoke into the phone as Aiden indicated to turn left, his mate was close, he could sense her more clearly now. "Aiden, drive a little way up the road and then turn around," he directed.

"Who's going to swap cars?" Caleb asked.

"The children and Katrina need to get in here. I'll get in the car with Belle." He would prefer for Belle to ride in the truck with Aiden, but it was risky putting all of Belle's family in one car with Aiden in case the pursuers realized what they'd done.

"We'll come with you," Elise offered.

"Elise, I don't want you..." Caleb was silenced by a sidelong look from his mate.

"We'll get out of the back seat and they can slide into our places," Elise said. "Aiden and Flora can protect them if they get followed."

"Agreed," Flora said. "We'll split up. If they follow you, we'll just head to Wishing Moon Bay. If they follow us, you'll need to turn around and come after us."

"That's a good plan," Aiden replied. "Although, if they do follow Belle's car, I'd rather be there when they catch up with you." He snarled under his breath, his shoulders tensed, and the whites of his knuckles showed as he twisted his fingers on the steering wheel.

If only he could wring the necks of the people chasing Belle and her family. He'd soon teach them not to threaten his mate and her kids. They were his to protect.

"I'll feel better knowing you and Flora are keeping the children safe," Rift replied.

"Do you think those people have anything to do with..." Caleb glanced down at the phone in Rift's hand, realizing that Katrina was still on the other end of the line.

"We'll ask them if they catch up with us," Rift replied.

"I'd sure be happy to force the information out of them with my fists." Caleb's lip turned up at the corner. "Or maybe I should introduce them to my bear. He's not in the mood to ask nicely."

"Okay, let's calm down a little," Elise said warily. "Don't go doing anything stupid. Just keep your cool."

Elise slipped her arm around Caleb's shoulder and he leaned on her, before kissing her cheek. "Don't worry. I'm in control."

"Good." She placed her hand on his cheek and turned him to face her, brushing her lips across his.

Rift licked his lips, he longed to taste his mate, to feel the warmth of her body as he held her in his arms. Was this fate's way of bringing them back together? If it was, he'd rather his mate had come back into his life without the threat of danger looming over her.

"Are you still there?" he asked Katrina.

"Still here. We're close to the end of the road. Still no sign of the other truck. I hope we haven't gotten you involved for nothing," she replied.

"It's better to be safe," Rift answered.

Maybe they were just opportunist guys, his snow leopard said. *The best result here would be for them to have given up and gone back to whichever rock they crawled out from under, while we still get to be the hero for our mate.*

You're right. But we don't know anything for sure. His jaw clenched. *What if they know where Belle lives?*

We'll go home with them, his snow leopard announced. *Until we know for sure the threat has passed, we won't leave their side.*

Belle might need some convincing about that idea, Rift said. *She might be suspicious of us and think we are involved in some way.*

How can we be involved? His snow leopard frowned.

It might seem suspicious that we showed up at the house and then these guys chased them. She might think we're in on it together. Rift would not blame her for suspecting them.

She wouldn't have called if she believed that, his snow leopard insisted.

You're right. I'm just afraid we might blow this one chance of winning our mate over. Rift focused on the road ahead as they passed a sign indicating the mountain road was close.

Then we'd better not blow it. His snow leopard was ready to move, ready to fight. Ready to make their mate see she needed him in their lives.

"This is it." Aiden leaned forward and peered ahead as they turned onto the road that ran along the side of the mountain. "I think I see them."

"You do?" Flora leaned forward. "Damn, you have good eyesight."

"Okay, swing the truck around, we'll wait for them here." Rift stared ahead of them. Aiden was right, up ahead a car was speeding toward them, although he couldn't make out the details yet, it had to be them.

Aiden pulled across the road before turning the wheel hard as he backed up the truck. Another couple of tries and he'd turned the truck around, Rift unclipped his seatbelt and turned to look out of the back window.

"Are you ready?" Caleb asked Elise.

"Yes." She unclipped her seatbelt and looped the strap of her purse over her head. "Should we get out now?"

"No, wait until the car slows down." Rift replied. "If there's a problem and they don't stop, we'll be ready to follow them."

He pushed his senses out, searching for his mate. She was there, in the car, the space between them growing less with each passing second. He could sense the other people in the car, the people he'd sworn to protect.

Then he pushed his senses out farther. If the truck was following them, he should be able to sense them, too. He closed his eyes briefly, pushing himself harder as his mind fought to cling to the presence of his mate. He wanted to blot out everything else and just focus on her. She was all that mattered.

Not true, his snow leopard stated. Her family matters, too. Katrina, Jack, and Rosie need to be kept safe, too.

Of course, they do. With a jolt, he let go of his mate and searched a wider area. *There, I can sense them. Four people coming this way.* He brought his awareness back to the truck.

"They're slowing down," Caleb cracked the back passenger door open. "We're going to need to act fast, the truck isn't far behind."

"You can sense them, too?" Rift asked.

Of course they can, his snow leopard replied drily.

"Yeah. Part of me is tempted to stay here and face them head-on, ask them what they're doing," Caleb admitted, his fists clenched.

"But that's not the part that's in control," Elise pushed him toward the door. "We just need to keep Belle and her family safe. No heroics, thank you."

"Elise is right," Rift agreed. "Although it's hard to fight the need to stop them right here, right now and sort the situation out. I don't want Belle and her family to be running forever."

"They won't if they come with us to Wishing Moon Bay," Flora said.

"No, they won't. But as much as I want Belle and her family to come with me back home, this isn't the way I want it to be. I want them to choose to be there. It's the only way they'll ever be happy." Rift nodded to Caleb who slid out of the truck, Elise followed.

Flora placed her hand over Rift's as he moved to follow the others. "She will make that choice one day, Rift. I'm sure of it."

He gave a tight smile and nodded. "I can only hope you're right."

Aiden glanced over his shoulder, his hands still gripped the steering wheel. "Flora is always right." He winked and inclined his head toward the door. "Now, get going. Go be a hero."

"Thanks." Rift choked down the lump of emotion in his throat. "I couldn't ask for a better family than you guys."

"Yeah, you could," Aiden said. "They're right there. Now go help them."

Rift slid out of the truck as Belle slowed the car to a stop. With a deep breath, he leaped into action. There wasn't much time.

He would keep them safe. No matter what.

9

BELLE

"Are we sure this is a good idea?" Belle slowed the car to a stop next to Aiden's truck.

"I'm not sure of anything right now," Katrina answered. "But if you're asking if we should trust these guys to help us, then yes."

"Why? Because we don't have any choice?" Were they being manipulated into splitting up? What if this whole thing was a ruse?

"Partly. And partly because Rift is the real deal." Katrina gathered up her purse and turned to look over her shoulder at the children in the back seat. "Are we ready to go on an adventure?"

"Where are we going?" Jack asked suspiciously, his video game stashed in his backpack which lay next to him on the back seat.

"We're going for a ride in that truck." Katrina pointed to the truck that was stopped on the side of the road about two hundred feet ahead.

"Why?" Jack looked mutinous. "Why aren't we staying with Mom?"

"Because you'll be safer in the truck." Belle adjusted her focus on the rearview mirror and looked beyond the two children in the back of the car. So far there had been no sign of the other truck since they'd turned around. Perhaps they'd given up.

Maybe Katrina was wrong and this whole thing was a robbery, nothing more. They'd thought that the passengers in the car would be easy pickings. But once Belle had turned around and driven off, they'd given up.

If so, was it a good idea to let her mom and children get in the truck with strangers?

"We should just keep on driving." Belle didn't take her foot off the accelerator.

Katrina placed her hand over the mouthpiece of the phone which she still held to her ear. "We're not taking any chances. Those guys meant business. Did you see the eyes of the one in the passenger seat?"

Belle glanced at her mom, the fear in her eyes was real. "Okay." She shook her head. "You're right. But I still don't like it."

"We can see you," Katrina spoke to Rift and then nodded. "Slow down, they're getting out of the truck." She pointed as three people got out and stood behind the vehicle.

"Mommy, I don't want to go," Rosie wailed.

"Rosie, please. Grandma will be with you." Belle used her not-open-to-negotiation voice. "We'll get ice cream as soon as this is over. Okay?"

Rosie pouted as she nodded.

"I'm staying with you." Jack folded his arms, his mind made up.

"No, you're going with Grandma and Rosie. I need you to keep them safe." Belle took her foot off the accelerator and eased down on the brake, she didn't want to stop too fast and skid across the road.

"We need you to take care of us, Jack. Can you do that for Grandma?" Katrina half-turned in her seat to face her grandson.

"I guess," Jack replied petulantly.

"Okay. Seatbelts off." Belle stopped the car and turned around to help the kids and as she did so, the passenger door flew open. Rift leaned into the car and hooked his hands under Rosie's arms. Belle's immediate reaction was to tell him to get his hands off her daughter. However, the tender expression on his face robbed her of words.

"Okay, Rosie. You are going for a ride in my brother's truck." He lifted her out and she threw her arms around his neck, clinging onto him as if it were the most natural thing in the world.

"Belle." Her mom's hand dragged her attention away. "I have my phone. We'll keep in touch. It'll be okay."

"Take care of them, Mom." Belle's eyes swam with tears that she quickly brushed away. This is not the time to cry, she needed to keep it together. But watching her children as they were bundled into the back of Aiden's truck, followed by her mom, made it difficult.

This was wrong. It was all so wrong. She should be with her kids.

"We need to go." Rift yanked open the passenger door and slid into the seat.

"They're getting close." Caleb climbed into the back seat with Elise next to him.

"Can you sense them?" Belle put the car in drive but didn't move until the truck containing her family drove off.

"We can. They're close, they'll be in view soon." Rift buckled his seatbelt and placed his hands on his thighs.

Belle pressed down on the accelerator and the car crept forward. "We should make sure they see which way we go."

"Aren't we trying to outrun them?" Elise asked.

"If they don't see which way we are going, they might go in the same direction as the truck." Belle neared the turn. The truck took a left and as they drove away, she was struck by the overwhelming sense of loss. She should be with them. How could she put her faith in a bunch of strangers?

"Belle's right." Rift's gentle reassuring smile made her heart flutter and chased her fear away.

"Okay. I told you I was ready to fight," Caleb said. "We could always force them out of the truck now."

"No!" Elise and Rift chorused. "Let's stick to the plan."

"Maybe Caleb is right. I need to know what they're doing. I need to know why they are after us."

"Not here." Rift shook his head. "We want to put some distance between us and your family."

"I checked out the map," Elise began. "Aiden's going left and heading for Wishing Moon Bay. We're going right. If we drive for approximately five miles, there's a road we can take that leads nowhere. If they follow us, that would be the perfect place for an ambush of our own."

"An ambush of our own?" Caleb didn't hide the shock from his voice.

"Yes." Elise half-turned to look at him. "You said there were four people in the truck behind us, right?"

"Yes," Caleb answered.

"You don't like those odds, considering we have two shifters and a fae?" Elise leveled her gaze at him.

"We don't know if any of the people in the truck are shifters," Rift reminded her.

"True. But I still like those odds. Plus, it means Belle and her family won't be on the run for the rest of their lives." Elise glanced at Belle. "Sorry, I should be more tactful."

"It's okay, you haven't said anything I haven't thought about myself." She'd stopped at the end of the road, not yet turning right as she watched in the rearview mirror for the truck to come into view. "There they are."

"Okay, go," Rift instructed and waved his hands forward as if that would make her go any faster.

Belle eased her foot down on the accelerator and gripped the steering wheel tightly as adrenaline pumped through her body once more. She was exhausted, her shoulders ached after fighting to control the car at such a high speed on a winding road. The added stress of her family being in trouble caused the pounding beat in her temple to increase, but she ignored it despite rising nausea caused by her headache.

She had to stay strong, she had to stay in control.

"Thank you." She glanced at Rift as she pressed down hard on the accelerator. They needed to keep a good distance between them and the truck behind, while also making sure they didn't lose them, if they were to follow Elise's plan.

"I told you, I'm here to protect you." Rift lowered himself down in his seat and angled his head so he could watch the truck as it reached the end of the road.

Belle held her breath as she glanced in the rearview mirror. If the truck turned left and followed Aiden and her family, she'd have to turn around. *Follow us. Follow us.* The words beat to the same rhythm as the blood thumping in her temples.

"Are they coming this way?" The road curved around to the left and she could no longer see the truck. "Can you tell? With your senses?"

Rift nodded and sat up a little straighter in his seat. "They're coming this way."

Elise and Caleb sank down in the back seat. "We'd better look like children and not adults."

"If they are shifters, will they be able to tell that you're not children?" Belle kept looking in the rearview mirror, waiting for the truck to catch them up. Would they try ramming the car off the road? Surely it was too exposed here with cars passing in the other direction.

"Possibly. It's not an easy thing to tell. The main problem is they might be able to tell if we're shifters. If they risk getting that close." He turned around in his seat. "I think we need to go with Elise's plan."

Caleb sucked in a deep breath and nodded. "You're right. But we need to make sure it doesn't look too obvious."

"How much farther?" Rift asked Elise.

"A couple of miles." Elise showed him the map on her phone.

"We need to go faster," Rift told Belle. "We need to look as if we're trying to outrun them. If not, it's going to look pretty obvious that we're trying to lure them off the road."

"Okay." She nodded and pressed her foot down on the gas. The car leaped forward, it was easier to drive faster on the more open road but there were still plenty of twists and turns that might hide danger.

"Great. You're doing great," Rift told her.

"That's not how I feel," she admitted. "Where are they taking the kids and my mom?"

"Aiden and Flora are taking them to Wishing Moon Bay. It's where we live. They'll be safe there, I promise." Rift kept his attention fixed on the road behind.

"Wishing Moon Bay. I've never heard of it. Is it far?" Panic rose inside her. Had she made a mistake? What if this was all part of their plan? Was she the one heading into an ambush?

"It's a couple of hours away. Our mom owns a hotel there. They'll be safe. Our brothers are there. They'll protect them," Rift assured her.

"More brothers?" Belle asked. "How many are there?" Although she was happy the rest of her family would be safe.

If she could trust these people.

"Six. Our mom, Valerie, adopted us when we were young. She's the only mother we've really known. She's one of the kindest people you could ever meet." Rift swallowed hard. He obviously loved his mom.

"That's good to know." Her jaw tensed. "I just want this over with."

"I know." He lifted his hand and reached for her but then changed his mind and placed it back down on his thigh before looking in the side mirror once more. "I can see them. I can sense them."

"The turn off the road is about a mile up ahead," Elise said. "The road curves right and then left. If you speed up a little more, it'll seem like you're trying to outrun them."

"If I get too far ahead, they'll miss me turning off the road." Belle pushed the car to go faster.

"Once they find out they've lost you, they'll double back." Rift kept watching in the mirror. "Or, if they turn off right after us, we'll know at least one of them are shifters."

"So, right now, they can sense us just like you can sense them." Belle nodded, of course, they would. She still couldn't get her head around the idea of shifters. But she couldn't deny what her eyes had seen.

What was weirder? That shifters could change from a person to an animal, or that they had super senses. Each was unnatural to her. Yet perfectly natural to them. As natural as walking and talking.

She ran her hand through her hair. This day was the craziest day of her life. Even crazier than the day Landon had told her he was leaving her and the kids. She'd always figured that would be the worst day of her life. Now, she wasn't so sure.

"Are you okay?" Rift asked.

She blinked. "Yes."

"Only you're easing off the gas." He nodded toward her foot on the pedal.

"I'm worried I'm going to go around one of these bends and crash into something," she admitted but only to excuse her lack of concentration.

"There's no one in front of us. At least not a person or another vehicle," he assured her.

"And you would know that because of your senses." She nodded. "They are handy, that's for sure."

"Okay, here on the left. Two hundred feet. One hundred feet," Elise sounded like a sat nav as she guided Belle to the turnoff. "There."

Belle took her foot off the gas and touched the brake, slowing down enough to take the corner without skidding across the road. Her car handled it perfectly. As she straightened the wheel, she pushed down on the gas. They needed to be out of sight of the road before the truck passed them by.

"I can sense them. They're close." Rift turned around in his seat and stared out of the back window even though he said he could sense them. Caleb and Elise did the same as Belle kept her eyes on the narrow road ahead.

"They went past." Caleb turned to face his brother. "We need a plan."

Belle slowed down as they got to the end of the road, which ended in a trail that led into the surrounding forest. As she steered the car around in a circle, her passengers devised a plan to take down the guys who had been following Belle and her family.

"Okay. Rift and I will get out of the car and head back up the road. When they come, we'll follow behind and make sure they can't escape." Caleb looked at them each in turn. "Elise, you and Belle wait in the car." He held up his hand as Elise was about to protest. "Please, you need to stay with Belle. You are our last line of defense."

Elise rolled her eyes. "Like if anyone can get past you two, I'd be able to take them down."

"If there are four of them, there's a chance one might get past us. If so, I am confident my fae mate will take him out." Caleb leaned forward and kissed her cheek, but Elise grabbed a hold of him and kissed his lips.

A small smile slid across Rift's face as he turned away to give the couple some privacy. As he moved, he locked eyes with Belle. How she longed to let her guard down and give in to this mating bond.

What would it be like to trust in fate, to become the mate of the man who was seated next to her?

A man who would risk everything for her.

After this was over, perhaps it was time to find out.

10

RIFT

"They're coming." Rift's words were met by a sharp intake of breath from Belle, while Elise and Caleb finally broke their kiss.

"Are you sure?" Belle's face paled. "Of course you're sure."

She trusts us, at last, Rift's snow leopard told him.

She does, Rift agreed. When they'd first met up with Belle and her family as they escaped the people after them, Rift was certain she thought this might be a setup.

She was wary of them. And she had every right to be, for all she knew they were playing her.

Now, she looked at him with trust in her eyes.

If only we knew what these guys wanted, Rift's snow leopard said as he and Caleb got out of the car.

It must have to do with Reggie, Rift answered. *But what?* There had been no time for discussions after they had swapped places with Belle's family. But, depending on the outcome of this fight, they would have to try to figure it out.

If we can get hold of one of the men, I can make him talk, the snow leopard was confident in his claim.

Oh, we'll make them talk, Rift assured him. This ends today.

Although, there was no certainty of that. These men might be hired thugs sent by someone else. Someone who meant Belle and her family harm.

It made little sense since Reggie was dead. Why would someone want to hurt them?

Why did Murray take the twins after their parents were dead? His snow leopard had a point.

But why after all this time? Why after Reggie died?

Maybe there's something in the house they want. His snow leopard flicked his tail angrily.

Rift glanced at the trunk of the car. Was that the answer? Did the car contain something they wanted? If so, would it be easier for them to simply hand it over and be done with the whole thing? *Unless it's something of sentimental value.* He looked at Belle through the windshield as he joined Caleb in front of the car.

It's too late to ask. He sniffed the air. They were close. Something was close.

Rift swung his head around to check on Caleb. His brother had sensed it, too.

"Something is coming through the trees." Rift moved to the left, heading toward whatever was coming their way.

However, Caleb put a hand on his shoulder and stopped him from moving any farther. "I'll go." He sniffed the air. "If I'm not mistaken, it's a bear. And no offense, but your snow leopard might not be a match for it."

"Should we split up at all?" Rift asked. "What if that's what they want? What if they figured out what we planned?"

Caleb turned his head from side to side, then a smile crept over his lips and he relaxed. "I don't think we have to worry."

"What?" Rift bent forward and turned his head from side

to side as he zoned in on the bear coming toward them. "Aiden?"

"Yeah." Caleb thumbed toward the car. "At least Belle can stop worrying that he's run off with her mom and kids."

Rift nodded. "I got the impression she wasn't too sure about us when we swapped places with the kids."

"Do you blame her?" He nodded in the direction of Aiden. "I'll go meet him. We should stick with the plan, it'll be easier with Aiden's help. I don't feel so outnumbered."

Rift nodded and as Caleb ran to the left to meet his twin, Rift headed to the right, melting into the trees. Only when he was completely out of view from the road and the oncoming truck did he shift into his snow leopard and slink back toward the road.

The truck was close now, the four people still inside. He was certain none of them were shifters, but he wasn't ready to take any chances. Moving at a jog now, he moved farther away from Belle's car, even though it went against everything he believed in.

He should be there with his mate. He should be by her side, protecting her. That was his job. That's what he'd promised he'd do.

Yet he had to stick to the plan. Even with Aiden's help, things could spiral out of control.

The snow leopard stopped and pushed his senses out as far as he could, stretching his limits. There was no one else around. Wait. Yes, there was. He could sense four other people, huddled together.

Flora, and Belle's family, were just within his range. He let out a sigh of relief, at least he wouldn't have to worry about them.

Although, that might expose them to danger if any of the guys in the truck was a shifter.

If Rift could sense Belle's family, then they might, too.

The truck passed Rift, who hid behind the dense undergrowth. They were going slow, no doubt looking into the forest for any sign of Belle's car.

Rift searched for his brothers. Caleb was matching the truck's speed, mirroring its movements as they closed in on Belle. Aiden was across the road, heading straight for Rift.

Rift waited for his brother to join him before they both shifted back into their human forms.

"Belle's mom kept telling us we shouldn't leave you guys. When Elise texted Flora to say the truck was following you, we decided to double back," Aiden explained. "In case you couldn't handle the situation by yourselves."

"I'd like to think we could, but honestly, I'm glad to have you here." Rift clapped his brother on the back. "Let's go see what these guys want."

They jogged along the edge of the road. Caleb still followed the truck, keeping parallel to the road as he traveled through the trees.

"Did Belle give you any clue?" Aiden asked.

"No, what about Katrina?" Rift asked. "Did she give anything away? Do you think she knows more about Reggie and Murray than she let on?" Rift didn't believe Katrina would do anything to hurt her daughter or the children. She obviously loved them and had raised Belle away from Reggie and Murray.

"Perhaps. There's a chance she might not want Belle to know some of the things her father was into. But I do believe her when she said she had no idea that Murray was into kidnapping children." Aiden stopped walking and stared at the truck in front of them. "But these guys might. These guys might be wrapped up in the whole thing."

"Maybe there was something in the house they wanted?" Rift asked. "Stolen goods?"

"That would be my guess. But looking at the house Reggie

was living in before he died, it doesn't look as if he had much money." Aiden raised an eyebrow at Rift. "There seemed little of value there. Perhaps if there was something, he sold it to give himself some cash to spend."

"You're right." He inclined his head toward the truck. "Caleb's about to make his move." Rift paused. "We should get closer. If we keep just inside the tree line, we'll be out of sight."

"Let's do it." Aiden kept low as they drew closer to the truck, making sure they could not be seen in the mirrors. They should be out of sight unless someone turned and looked directly at them.

Caleb emerged from the trees and stepped out in front of the truck, which abruptly stopped, the guys in the front leaning sharply forward as the brakes were slammed on. For a moment, no one in the truck moved, they simply stared at Caleb before exchanging startled glances with each other.

Aiden and Rift drew level with the doors, ready to deal with anyone who left the truck if they caused trouble. The plan was to let the guys talk so they could learn why they were here and exactly what they wanted from Belle and her family.

"Here we go." Rift tensed as the passenger door opened and two guys got out of the truck.

"There are another two men in the truck," Aiden murmured. "I'll watch them while you stick with these two."

"Agreed." Rift shadowed the two men as they closed the truck door and moved toward Aiden.

"What do you want, *friend*?" The first guy was about six feet tall, broad-shouldered, and with the confidence of a man who knew how to handle himself.

"I could ask you the same thing." Caleb kept his tone light and friendly, but Rift knew his brother too well. There was an underlying steeliness to his voice, a warning to back off.

The guys didn't. Instead, they drew level with the hood of the truck, closing the gap between them and the bear shifter. "We need to talk with the people in that car there. So, step away and don't get involved in something that doesn't concern you."

The second guy suddenly broke away from the first and ran toward the car. Rift's reflexes kicked in and he sprinted forward, grabbing the guy around the shoulders, and despite being smaller and lighter, wrestled him to the ground.

The guy struggled, breaking free of Rift's hold to land a punch on his jaw. Rift reeled back, clenched his fist, and threw a punch, whacking the guy in the temple. He smacked into the ground, his head ricocheting off the hard road. He didn't get back up.

Rift checked the passengers in the car, using his senses to locate his mate and Elise. Happy they were safe, he wheeled around and ran back to the truck. One of the other passengers had attempted to get out but Caleb slammed the truck door his legs, preventing him from going to the aid of his friends.

Meanwhile, Aiden was dueling with the first guy, exchanging blows. They were evenly matched in size and strength, but the guy seemed to have had training. His footwork was light and controlled, like a professional boxer.

As they fought, the driver of the truck suddenly slammed his foot on the accelerator, and the vehicle jolted forward, aiming straight for Belle's car.

The guy who Rift had knocked out woke up, startled eyes popped from his pale face as he scurried out of the way. Rift sprang after the truck, helpless to stop the vehicle as it sped toward his mate.

The doors of the car were flung open as Elise and Belle rushed to safety. But as soon as Belle was out of the car, the guy Rift had hit propelled himself forward and grabbed her by the wrist. She yelped and brought her knee up to his groin, but he spun her around and closed his arms around her body, leaving her gasping for air.

"Let's all just take a moment, shall we?" the guy snarled as he grabbed Belle's wrist and twisted it cruelly. She cried out, leaving Rift fighting with his other side as his snow leopard fought for freedom, fought for the right to finish this guy who dared hurt their mate.

Behind Rift, Aiden let go of the man he'd fought and nearly overpowered, while Caleb stalked forward to stand at Rift's shoulder. He had his brother's back as always.

"Let her go," Rift ordered.

"Not until we get what we came for," the guy said.

"What did you come for?" Belle asked.

Elise kept low and moved to hide behind the car as the guy jerked Belle upward. "You know what I want. The treasure."

"Treasure?" Belle asked. "What treasure?"

"Reggie kept it hidden all these years. But he had it all along. We knew you'd lead us to him eventually."

"Reggie is dead," Belle spat. "He's cold in the ground and the only things he left behind are in the trunk of my car, and believe me, there is no treasure there. It's all junk."

"You expect me to believe that?" the guy asked.

"Why would I lie?" Belle asked.

"Because it's in your blood. Your father was a murderer. Your uncle was a murderer." He took a long shuddering breath. "We know what they did. We know they have dragon blood on their hands. And unless you hand over the treasure, you do, too."

"Dragon blood?" She gasped as the shock of his words hit her. "I don't know what you mean."

Rift made his move, but the guy stared directly at him and shook his head as he tightened his grip further.

A flash of movement from behind the car caught his eye as he looked on helplessly while the guy held his mate prisoner. Elise.

She sprang forward and spun around, the thick tree branch in her hands aimed at the guy's head. A sickening crack and the branch exploded, felling the guy who sank to his knees.

Belle ran forward and Rift opened his arms, needing to feel her safely in his embrace.

A shout from behind them and the truck plunged forward again. Rift, his arms locked around his mate, leaped to the side as the truck grazed the car's hood. One of the guys got out of the truck and dragged their fallen friend to his feet. The others helped, getting him into the back seat of the truck.

"We know where you live!" someone yelled. "Give us the treasure and you can go on with your lives. The choice is yours."

The truck doors slammed, and wheels kicked up damp leaf mold as they backed away, heading back up the road.

Rift watched them go, his arms still wrapped around Belle as they lay on the ground. She didn't struggle for freedom, instead, she lay limp, breathing harshly as she gasped for air.

"Are you okay?" He moved, loosening his hold as he gently turned her over.

"Yeah, I'm okay," she rasped. "It's just my wrist that hurts."

"Wait, I have something that'll help." Elise ran to the car and returned with her purse. Rummaging inside, she pulled out a small jar and twisted it open. "I always carry it for emergencies. It's a special mix, arnica and some other herbs. It'll help with the bruising."

Rift clenched his fists as Elise lathered the cream onto Belle's wrist. The marks where the guy had twisted it viciously were red and angry. He wanted to shift and run after the truck. He wanted to track them down and maim them for life for hurting his mate.

But he needed to be here with his mate. She needed him more than he needed revenge.

11

BELLE

Belle touched her wrist, the pain was subsiding. "Thanks." She nodded at Elise.

"You're welcome. When we get back to Wishing Moon Bay, I'll treat the bruising with something stronger." Elise glanced at Rift and then went to join Caleb and Aiden.

"I'm sorry." Rift's mouth turned up at one corner. "I promised to protect you and...you got hurt."

"This is not your fault." She pointed to her wrist. "You didn't do this, they did." She took a deep breath that shuddered through her body. "Whoever they were."

"Do you have any idea what they want?" Rift asked. "Any clue as to what this treasure is?"

She shook her head. "No." She glanced over his shoulder, staring down the road, worried they might come back. "But my mom thinks she recognized the one guy. He went to her house asking about Reggie."

"Reggie." Rift nodded. "He must have stolen something from them and now they want it back. Do you have any idea what it could be? Was there anything in Reggie's belongings they might mean?"

"Everything from the house is packed into the back of the car." She turned around, her legs weak as she walked to the trunk and opened it. "It's not a lot, we were going to take anything salvageable to the thrift store and the rest is heading for the trash."

"When we get to Wishing Moon Bay, we should go through it all and check that there's nothing we've missed." Rift stared at the boxes. Did he also have X-ray vision? Could he see the contents of the boxes through the thick cardboard?

"I never said I was going to Wishing Moon Bay." Belle folded her arms across her body as Rift turned around to face her.

"You'll be safe there."

"For how long? If we run now, we'll be running forever." She jutted her chin out, she appreciated his help, but he wasn't the person to make decisions for her and her family.

"Belle, those guys are out there, they know where you live, they know where Katrina lives, and they know how to handle themselves." He reached out and placed his hand on her upper arm. Warmth flooded her body, a comforting warmth that lulled her into believing this would all work out if they stuck together.

She didn't need a savior.

"I know all that. But we have a life here. When we get back home, I'll call the police." Even in her head, her idea sounded lame.

"They can't watch over you all the time. These guys have been waiting for how many years for Reggie to find this treasure?" Every word Rift said was true. And she hated it.

Ever since Landon had left her to raise Jack and Rosie alone, she'd relied on herself. And Katrina, of course, but her mom was independent, too. Growing up, Belle's mom had shown her how to cope and deal with her own problems.

Belle wasn't ready to hand over control to someone else. Yet Rift was right, they were not safe.

"And what happens when we go to Wishing Moon Bay?" She unconsciously closed her hand over her sore wrist, which was a constant reminder of the attack.

A constant reminder that until they resolved this, neither Belle nor her family were safe.

"We figure this out so you can go back to your lives." His gentle smile assured her they'd figure it all out.

Belle nodded. "I should go talk to my mom. Maybe there's something she's forgotten. You know, from when my dad was alive. Before Reggie..." She covered her eyes with her hand as tears trickled down her cheeks. "Those poor kids."

"Not your fault." He ducked his head and took hold of her hand, pulling it away so he could look into her eyes. "Isn't that what you told me?"

She sniffed loudly and nodded. "You're right. I always remind myself that when I teach my kids life skills, I have to lead by example."

"You're a good mom, Belle." He placed his hand on the open trunk and slammed it shut. "We need to go." Rift looked along the road, his eyes out of focus.

"Are they coming back?" She took an involuntary step closer to him.

"No." He turned ninety degrees and stared into the surrounding trees. "You should call your mom and tell her everything is okay."

"Oh!" She pulled her phone out of her pocket. "Mom. It's me."

"Belle, I was about to get out of the truck and come find you. Are you okay?" Katrina paused. "Are you hurt?"

Belle glanced at her bruised wrist which still throbbed despite Elise's ointment. Rift's eyes lingered on her fingers as they stroked the bruised skin and his eyes darkened. "I'm okay. I just have a sore wrist."

"A sore wrist. What happened?" Katrina's voice rose in panic.

"I'll explain when I see you. Right now we need to get going." She paused and looked at Rift. This was it, decision time. Would her mom agree with going to Wishing Moon Bay?

"Are the men gone?" Katrina lowered her voice and whispered. "Are we safe?"

"For now." Belle swallowed hard as she fought to stop the threatening tears.

"What do we do?"

"We're going to Wishing Moon Bay. At least until we figure something out. The kids aren't at school for another week. Hopefully, it'll all be resolved by the time their new semester starts." Belle put her fingers to her temple and her headache had worsened as the shock of the attack weighed on her.

"I think that's for the best." Katrina sobbed down the phone. "I'm so sorry."

"This isn't your fault." She glanced at Rift who had walked around to the driver's side of the car. She was about to ask her mom if she had any idea what the men had been looking for. If she had any clue what the treasure was. But it was a conversation best left alone for now. Belle would speak to Katrina in private.

"I'll see you soon." Katrina ended the call and Belle slipped her phone into her pocket and went to join Rift. "What's the plan?"

"Shall I drive? You look all done in." His worry deepened the laughter lines around his mouth. "And you should rest your wrist."

"That might be a good idea. I have a headache from hell

and an adrenaline rush hangover. All I want to do is curl up in a ball and sleep." Belle rubbed the back of her neck. "I feel so damn useless."

"You're not useless. You've had a shock...or two today." Rift hooked his hand under her arm and led her around to the passenger side of the car. "Sit, try to relax."

"Wait." She didn't get in the car, instead, she headed over to where Caleb, Aiden, and Elise were talking quietly. "Thanks. For risking your lives for me. I don't know what I'd have done if you hadn't come back for us."

"You're family now." Elise slid her arms around Belle's shoulders and hugged her lightly. "Family sticks together."

Belle took a shuddering breath and dashed her hand across her eyes. "I'm used to doing things on my own. I'm used to being the person I depend on. Aside from my mom. It might take some getting used to."

"Then take your time, there's no rush." Elise rubbed her back. "Come on, you look as if you're about to keel over."

"Yeah. I feel it. But what about my mom and the kids?" Belle turned around and scanned the trees. "Is someone going to drive with them?"

"Flora is going to drive the truck to Wishing Moon Bay. We're going to squeeze in the car with you. We'll make sure that no one follows us." Rift guided her back to the car.

"Are they safe on their own?" Belle's concern grew.

"We won't be far behind them. But if those guys are watching us, it's best if we don't have contact with the truck." Rift put his hand on the door and helped her into the car.

"Can't Aiden go back to them through the trees?" She fastened her seatbelt and leaned her head back on the headrest.

"I could, but it's risky. And anyway, if they attack, we're certain they'll come at you again. And we might not be as lucky at fending them off," Aiden replied.

"Lucky." Elise put her hands together as if she were swinging a bat. "I took that guy out."

"You did." Caleb hooked his arm around her shoulders and pulled her close, planting a kiss on her cheek. "Remind me to never cross you."

"Ah, you never would. You're my mate." She slid her arms around his neck and kissed him, her body pressed tightly against Caleb's.

"Can you two get a room?" Aiden complained. "I don't want to sit in the back of the car with you two kissing all the way home."

Caleb chuckled. "Hey, you found your mate first. I had to put up with you and Flora kissing while I was alone."

"For a couple of days," Aiden said hotly.

"A couple of long days," Caleb complained as they all got in the back of the car.

"Your mom must be a brave woman to have raised six kids," Belle told Rift.

Rift nodded and chuckled as he started the engine. "Valerie is something special. We owe her so much."

"Is she going to be okay with you showing up with a family in tow?"

"She'll be so happy, she'll explode." Rift's smile widened. "She's always hoped that we'd all find mates. Now there's only Ivan left."

"Wow, he's the odd one out. That's going to be tough." Belle's eyes grew heavy as they left the forest road behind and headed toward Wishing Moon Bay.

Wherever that was.

As the wheels turned and the engine throbbed, she slipped under the veil of sleep.

Her future was uncertain, but she trusted Rift. She trusted his family.

They would protect her and the kids.

But would they ever be able to go back to their old life? And if they did, where did Rift fit into that? He obviously loved his family and his hometown. Would he give it all up for her?

As sleep finally claimed her, she realized she'd already accepted that he was a part of her life now. She was his mate, and they were meant to be together.

This sure was one crazy day. Or was it all a dream?

12

RIFT

Rift glanced at his mate, sleeping in the passenger seat beside him. She looked so serene, as if she didn't have a care, and he longed to make that a reality for her.

We will, his snow leopard assured him as they neared the turnoff to Wishing Moon Bay.

I sure hope there is something in those boxes in the trunk that'll give us some clue as to what those guys are after. If not, we're going to need a new plan. Rift checked the rearview mirror. They'd driven along this same stretch of road three times, each time the shifters had pushed out their senses to try to locate the truck or anyone else that might be following them.

At last, there was no one within a mile of them. It was time to go home.

Flora had already arrived in town, she'd gone there directly after the incident in the forest. As far as she could tell, there was no one following her, and she had taken the same precautions of looping back several times to check there was no one following the truck. It might have been overcautious since the guys in the truck had never seen

Aiden's vehicle. But overcautiousness was better than complacency.

If those guys found Wishing Moon Bay, Belle and her family might not be the only ones in danger.

Do you think those people were connected to what happened to Aiden and Caleb? His snow leopard asked the question that had been in Rift's mind for the whole trip. He'd turned it over and over in his head, but he had no answer.

I don't know. What are the chances of any of these being connected? Our mate and our brothers. It's like our lives are woven together so intricately.

Fate brought us together in the same way fate brings mates together, his other side mused.

Rift ran his hand through his hair. He was hungry and tired, verging on grouchy, but they would soon be home.

Elise had called ahead and asked Ivan to prepare some food for them. She hadn't said that Rift had found his mate. That was news Rift should break in person.

"Valerie is going to be super excited." Elise leaned forward and whispered in his ear so as not to wake Belle.

"She is." He couldn't help worrying about Ivan, though. Would the dragon shifter ever find his mate, or would he be forever alone?

Maybe his mate is on the dragon isle, his snow leopard suggested.

The one place he's not supposed to go, Rift replied.

One of the places he's not supposed to go. Valerie has always warned him about going into the fae realms, too. His snow leopard flexed his claws. Since two of our brothers have fae for mates, Ivan's mate might also be fae.

Great. That would incredibly unfair. Rift rubbed his hand over his chin. Ever since they were kids growing up in Wishing Moon Bay, Valerie had warned them not to go into the fae realm.

Fae didn't like shifters in general, but they had a particular dislike of dragon shifters.

Although Aiden and Caleb had traveled to the fae realm with their mates, Ivan had yet to set foot in the realms. Even talking about it made Valerie nervous.

She'd never told them why. It was one of many mysteries and the brothers respected Valerie's silence.

Their mom had only ever done what was best for her sons. She'd worked hard to raise them and keep them safe.

And fed. His snow leopard licked his lips. *I am hungry.*

We'll be there soon. Darkness surrounded them as they drove through the long narrow tunnel leading to Wishing Moon Bay.

Elise shuddered and sat back in her seat. "I don't know if I'll ever get used to this tunnel."

"Don't worry, I'm here for you." Caleb slipped his arm around her shoulder and pulled her close.

"I'm not scared," she told him even though she snuggled closer to him and rested her head on his shoulder. "I just don't like the dark, it kind of crowds in on you."

"Is it nighttime?"

Rift visibly jumped as Belle sat up straight in her seat and looked around. "No, we're in a long tunnel." He pointed ahead. "There's the end. Can you see the light?"

She yawned and leaned forward before she rubbed her eyes. "I see it." She yawned again. "Where are we?"

"We're just entering Wishing Moon Bay. The tunnel is the only road in and out." Rift glanced sideways at her even though he couldn't see her features in the dim light. But he didn't need light to picture her face. He'd memorized every curve, every line.

He ground his molars together as he recalled the vivid red marks left by the guy who had hurt her.

We owe Elise a debt, his snow leopard said. Without her, we could have lost our mate before we even had time to get to know her.

We do owe her. And one day we'll repay the debt. The end of the tunnel neared and as the light grew, Belle stared ahead, her eyes intense. She was the most beautiful woman he'd ever seen.

His breath caught in his throat. How had he gotten so lucky?

"I slept the whole trip?" Belle's voice wasn't as raspy after her sleep and as they emerged from the tunnel, he was grateful to see the marks had faded. Elise's ointment seemed to have done its job.

"You did. I figured it was better to let you sleep so you didn't worry about your family." He nodded ahead. "They're already in town, they should be at the hotel by now."

Belle ran her fingers through her tangle of hair which hung below her shoulders. She looked adorable, and he licked his lips as his eyes settled on her full lips. "I look a mess." She pulled down the sun visor and looked at herself critically in the mirror. "Urgh."

"Don't worry, you can get cleaned up when we get to the hotel. There's a hot meal waiting for us, too," Rift told her.

"Are the kids okay? Have you spoken to my mom?" Belle flipped the visor up.

"Aiden called Flora to check in on them a half-hour ago. Then your mom texted to say they had reached town. They seem fine, the kids think they're going on an adventure. Jack's extra happy because he overheard part of the conversation you had with your mom and he thinks he's not going back to school." Rift smiled to himself as Belle wriggled up in her seat.

"Does he? That is so like Jack."

"Doesn't he like school?" Rift asked.

"He says it's boring."

"I can relate to that. I always thought the world outside the classroom had more to teach me," Rift confessed.

Belle smiled and waggled her finger at him. "Please, do not repeat that in front of my son. It wouldn't take much for him to decide that he doesn't need school."

"Ah, I can help him there. It wasn't until I got a little older that I realized I needed school to teach me about the world outside of the classroom. We used to go on field trips to the beach and the mountains and I learned about the world and the creatures who live in it. I learned how the mountains were formed and how the moon pulls the oceans toward the shore." He blinked a couple of times. "Yeah, I liked school. Eventually."

"That does sound like the kind of school Jack would like. He loves the outdoors, but unfortunately, we live in a large town and we don't always have time to travel to wide open spaces. Which is a pity because he's a boy who likes to run." She turned her head and stared at the mountains in the distance. "It sure is beautiful here."

"It is." Rift nodded, wishing he could figure out how to make Belle see she could have a happy life here with him. She would be happy, the children would be happy.

And we would be ecstatic, his snow leopard said.

We would be in heaven, Rift agreed.

"So, you grew up in a hotel?" Belle dragged her attention away from the distant mountains.

"We did. Valerie had a large apartment next to the hotel and we all lived there. It's smaller now, she's downsized a lot since we all moved out. Most of the room has been given over to the restaurant. My brother, Ivan, is an amazing chef." His stomach rumbled just thinking about the food waiting for them at the hotel.

"A chef. I can't wait to try his food. I am hungry, it's been hours since we ate." Belle made a new attempt to tame her hair. "I wish I'd gotten some clean clothes and a hairbrush. Maybe you could sneak me in the back door or something."

"You're beautiful just the way you are." Rift glanced in the rearview mirror as Aiden covered his mouth to hide his smile. He'd almost forgotten they weren't in the car alone. Being so close to his mate made him forget about everyone and everything else.

"Did your mom teach you to be charming to women, too?" Belle's eyes danced as she teased him, and he was grateful to see her looking much more relaxed and at ease.

"Yes, she did. Along with always being polite and looking after each other. Family is important. We should always look out for each other." He pointed ahead. "There's the hotel. Aiden's truck is parked outside."

"Are the kids there? I can't see them." Belle sat up and wriggled in her seat until she was on the edge, staring at Aiden's truck.

"There they are." Elise checked her phone as a message came through. "It's Flora asking where we are." She leaned across Caleb, rolled down the window, and stuck her hand out, waving it frantically. "We're here."

Flora turned around and watched the car as Rift drove it into the parking lot and stopped next to the truck. He opened the door to get out, but Belle was faster. Even before the car stopped, she'd unfastened her seatbelt and thrown the door open so she could run for her kids with her arms open.

"I missed you, are you okay?" She knelt on the ground and scooped them up, clutching them to her as if they were the most precious things in the world.

They are, his snow leopard replied. To Belle, there's nothing more important than her children. Which is how it must be.

That's okay, I'm happy to be in second place to Rosie and Jack. Rift would happily be any place as long as Belle was by his side. He chuckled at his own joke as he got out of the car and closed the door.

"Hey, good to see you again, Katrina." Rift made a beeline for Belle's mom while his mate hugged the children so tightly Jack pretended to gasp for air.

"Not as good as it is to see you all." She reached out for Rift and hugged him tightly. "I don't know how to thank you for coming back for us."

"You know I'll always come if you need me," Rift assured her. "You know Belle is my mate."

"I know. I know. But part of me was scared that the mating bond wasn't all it was cracked up to be. It's one thing to hear about it, it's another to experience it. I'm just happy my daughter has you in her life." Katrina buried her face in his shoulder as Belle tilted her head back and looked up at him.

Do you think Belle has any doubts about how strong the mating bond is? His snow leopard was incredibly happy to have their mate here. After their earlier fear that she might walk out of their lives forever and never return, this was the best outcome they could have asked for. Which brought a huge dose of guilt along with it. They were only here in Wishing Moon Bay because they were in danger.

Rift would have preferred them to be here for happier reasons.

"There you all are." Valerie emerged from the hotel, her curious gaze resting on Belle and the children before switching to Rift who was still firmly clamped to Katrina.

"I heard we were having guests." Valerie walked down the steps to meet them, using her cane to keep herself balanced. A recent operation had left her stiff, but she was getting stronger and more like her usual self, more and more each day.

"More than guests," Aiden replied.

Valerie stopped walking, leaning heavily on her stick as she studied Rift. "You have news?" She glanced from Katrina to Belle and then her attention fixed on the children.

"I do." He let go of Katrina and moved toward Belle who stood up, holding her children's hands.

This is awkward, his snow leopard said, although he couldn't wait to break their happy news to Valerie.

"Hi." Belle nodded and stepped closer to Rift. "I'm Belle. And you must be Valerie. This is my mom, Katrina."

"Good to meet you, Katrina. There's food and coffee inside. Or tea if you prefer. Ivan's kept the kitchen open for you. It sounds as if you've had an adventure." Valerie smiled warmly at Katrina.

"Thank you. An adventure, that would be one way of putting it." Katrina aimed a concerned glance at Belle, her eyes resting on the fading marks on her daughter's wrist.

"And who are these little people?" Valerie smiled down at Jack and Rosie, her love for children evident as, despite her stiff leg, she lowered herself down to their height.

"This is Jack. And this is Rosie." Belle introduced her children, mirroring the same pride and love as Valerie had when she spoke about her children. Even though they hadn't been children for decades.

"Hello, Jack. Hello, Rosie. I'm Valerie. Do you want to come inside the hotel and see what we can find to eat?" Valerie leaned her weight on her stick as she straightened up.

"Hello. Are you Rift's mom?" Jack asked.

"I am," Valerie confirmed as her gaze switched from the children to rest on Belle's face for a moment. Then she glanced at Rift, who nodded, the unspoken message met with a wide smile from Valerie. Tears sparkled in her eyes as she took a long shuddering breath.

"Your hotel looks like a castle." Rosie tugged on Belle's hand, pulling her toward the hotel steps as she stared up at the turret that had sat on top of the hotel since it had been built.

"It does, doesn't it? Do you know it's one of the reasons I wanted to buy it? I always wanted to be a princess," Valerie confessed.

"Me, too!" Rosie replied.

"We're going to get along just fine." Valerie paused at the bottom of the steps and turned around, her expression unreadable as she took in the scene before her. Three of her beloved sons, all with their mates.

She's happy, his snow leopard sighed.

She isn't the only one, Rift replied lightly. We should make the most of this time and forget about the danger that stalked Belle, even if just for one day.

13

BELLE

"Do you need anything from the car?" Rift was by her side as she reached the steps to the hotel. He'd seemed tongue-tied when his mom had asked for introductions. After a fleeting moment of uncertainty, her fear that his mother might not approve of his mate already having two children was instantly swept aside.

"I have my purse. Rosie has her favorite toy and her favorite princess book, and Jack has his game console." A smile slipped across her lips. "You'll soon learn that these are the only necessities in the world. At least until Rosie moves on to a new favorite book."

"I'm looking forward to learning everything about you all." Color crept across his cheeks and her fondness for him deepened. She liked him. Unlike most of the other men she'd met, he genuinely wanted to get to know the family as a package deal.

"There's plenty you won't like," she assured him. "It's not all rainbows and unicorns, even in Rosie's world of princesses."

"I've grown up with five brothers. I know more than most

people how you have to learn to accept others and their faults while hoping they accept yours, too. Over time, we've worn down the sharp edges. But it has taken time, I'm not expecting to seamlessly slip into your lives." Rift took the steps two at a time and pulled open the door for his mom.

Belle followed, certain that if she let him, Rift would slip seamlessly into their lives. He was kind and patient and above all, loyal. If the shifter bond was true.

The whole thing was still a struggle to get her head around. But she wasn't going to question it. She wasn't going to push any boundaries, not when Rift had promised to keep them safe from whoever was out there hunting them.

She paused at the top of the steps, despite Jack and Rosie pulling her forward to enter the hotel. Her neck prickled as she looked out over the town.

Had the men in the truck managed to follow them despite their precautions?

The hotel lobby wasn't large, the reception desk, manned by a guy who studied them with some curiosity if not amusement, filled most of the room. But it was well maintained and clean, the decoration modern and yet in keeping with the outside of the building.

Tasteful. That would be her impression of the hotel. Tasteful and welcoming. The kind of place you could stay without having to feel awkward about saying the wrong thing or wearing the wrong clothes.

Belle relaxed a little more. The hotel confirmed her first impression of Valerie. Open and warm, the hotel reflected the woman who owned it and who had raised her adopted children under its roof.

"This way. We'll go through to the dining room. Rift, can you go to the kitchen with your brothers and bring the food? Ivan's in there but the rest of the serving staff have gone home." Valerie directed her sons and they obeyed, even though Rift lingered by her side for a couple of moments as if he didn't want to leave.

She liked that.

Damn, she was falling for him already. So much for putting her children first and giving up on romantic love until they were all grown up.

When Landon left, she'd promised herself she wouldn't expose her children to a string of broken relationships. She'd accepted, at least in the short term, that she would be single.

But she'd never factored meeting her mate into that relationship equation.

Meeting Rift had turned her whole life upside down. Not least because of the events that followed.

"It's okay." Katrina joined her as they entered the dining room. "I think we're all safe here."

Belle nodded.

"It's just you're gripping their hands so hard..." Katrina touched the back of Belle's hand.

"Sorry." She loosened her grip on Rosie, who looked up at her with eyes filled with wonder as she pointed out of the large window that ran along one side of the restaurant.

"Can we go look?" Rosie slipped out of her grasp. Her daughter hadn't even noticed the hold her mom had on her, she was so enraptured by the hotel.

"Sure." Belle let go of her children and a sudden sense of being alone hit her. She'd meant to make them feel safe, but that worked both ways. They gave her comfort and security. "Letting go is hard."

Katrina smiled sadly. "It's the hardest thing a mother ever has to do."

"Shall we sit here?" Valerie guided them to a table close to the window. "Flora, Elise, shall we push these together?"

"Yes, let's make one long table." Elise and Flora, under

Valerie's direction, reorganized the tables so that they could all sit in one big group.

"Is there anything we can help with?" Belle hated people waiting on her. Yet it was more than that. Her family was so small. She had no brothers and sisters, no cousins. Here, she already felt as if she was part of a larger family.

"No, you sit here." Valerie pulled out a chair and beckoned to her. "And your mom can sit next to you here. The boys are coming with the food."

Belle swapped smiles with her mom. She loved Valerie referring to her sons as boys even though they were all grown up. Katrina had often told Belle that she was her little girl even when she reached forty a couple of years back.

Shifter families were just like any other family.

Belle sat down but glanced at Valerie out of the corner of her eye. Was Valerie a shifter, too? Rift hadn't spoken much about them all. Not that they'd had a chance to talk since she'd slept the whole trip here.

"Mommy, can we go outside?" Rosie ran up to the table while Jack stayed by the window, staring out as a young boy of similar age played with his dad. A pang of longing hit Belle.

"Maybe later. First, we're going to eat." Belle looked up as the door opened and Rift appeared carrying two plates of food. It was as if she'd sensed his presence before the door opened. The mating bond worked both ways.

"Oh, the food smells wonderful." Katrina beckoned to Rosie. "Why don't you come and sit next to me? I'm sure we can go outside later."

"Okay." Rosie took her grandma's hand and scrambled up in the chair next to her. "Jack!" she called. "Food."

"Jack, honey, come on." Belle got up from her chair and went to fetch her son.

"I like it here," Jack told her as he followed her back to the table. "Can we live here?"

"Let's just focus on one thing at a time and right now that is eating." Belle pulled out a chair for her son, but he dodged around her.

"I'm going to sit next to Rosie." He dragged the chair out and sat down. Immediately, they started to talk in hushed whispers.

Jack and Rosie got along well, compared to their friends' brothers and sisters, who often seemed to be at war. They took care of each other and seldom argued. When they did argue, the dispute was usually settled before bedtime. Especially since their dad had left. It was as if they sensed they were more reliant on their mom and each other.

"These are for you, Belle and Katrina." Rift set the plates down in front of them. "And Caleb has smaller portions for the children."

"This smells wonderful." Katrina leaned forward and smelled the food. "Spaghetti and meatballs."

"The meatballs are flavored with herbs I gathered from the wildwood," Elise told them.

"Elise works with me in the kitchen, when she's not off on some adventure in the world beyond." A tall man, not as broad-chested as Aiden and Caleb, entered the restaurant carrying more plates.

"This is my brother Ivan," Rift introduced.

"Hi. Thanks for feeding us," Belle began as the expression on Ivan's face changed from friendly to hostile. His nostrils flared and he practically dropped the plates he was carrying on the table as his eyes widened and he swung his head toward Rosie.

"Ivan." Rift placed his hand on his brother's arm as he leaned forward.

"What's wrong?" Belle rose from her seat and went to her

daughter who hadn't noticed the apparent threat as she talked to Jack.

"I..." Ivan looked tortured and confused as he breathed heavily, his gaze fixed on Rosie.

"Perhaps we should go." Belle's throat constricted. Was nowhere safe for them?

"No." Ivan shook his head as he stepped backward, even though it seemed to take all his self-control to move away.

"Ivan, what's wrong?" Valerie got up and went around the table to her son.

"There's something...I can feel it." His eyes darkened and sweat appeared on his forehead.

"Rosie, what do you have there?" Katrina reached across her granddaughter. "Show me?"

"It's nothing." Rosie shoved something into the pocket of her jacket.

"Rosie." Belle got out of her seat and went to her daughter, crouching down by her side. Her heart raced and bile rose in her throat. "Show me what you have. It's important."

"It's just playing dress-up," Rosie stated as she looked at Jack.

"We found it in the backyard when you were talking," Jack said defensively.

"What did you find?" Belle held out her hand. "It's important."

Rosie locked eyes with her mom for a long moment. "I didn't steal it."

"It was under a bush in the yard," Jack added. "Wrapped in a towel. We figured it was treasure and whoever finds treasure can keep it, right?"

Treasure. Belle half-turned, her eyes locked with Rift's for a moment. His attention was fixed on her, while his fingers were tightly wrapped around his brother's arm. She blinked and turned back to her daughter. "I need to see it. It might belong to someone else. They might be looking for it."

They might do bad things to people to get it back. She swallowed her fear, her bruised wrist reminding her of the bad things that could happen to her or her family.

Had Jack and Rosie found what those people were looking for?

"It's not always that simple," Belle said gently. "Someone else might have buried it there. Or it might have been stolen and we need to figure out who it belongs to and give it back."

Rosie pouted as she listened. "But someone left it in the dirt, and we cleaned it. Why would they have left it there if they wanted it?"

"I don't know. But think of it this way..." Belle formulated her words in a way Rosie would understand. "What if you lost Jazzy?" Belle waggled the doll's arm as she rested in Rosie's lap. "If someone found her, you would want them to try to find out who she belonged to, wouldn't you?"

"Yes." Rosie's arm tightened around her most prized possession.

"She might be treasure to someone else and you would be sad if they kept her and didn't try to find out who she belonged to." Belle stroked Rosie's face as her eyes filled with tears. "Do you understand why you have to give what you found to me so we can try to find the owner?"

Rosie nodded and reached into her pocket, withdrawing the treasure, a jewel-encrusted tiara. No wonder Rosie had thought it was a dress-up item. It looked similar to some of the things she had in her dress-up box. However, when she placed it in her mom's hand, Belle intuitively knew she was not holding a cheap toy.

"If we don't find the owner, can I have it back?" Rosie asked.

"We'll see. I can't promise you, Rosie." She kissed her daughter's cheek and stood up.

As she ran her thumb over the large blue jewel set on the top of the tiara, she was convinced this was the treasure those guys were looking for.

However, as she looked up, her eyes locked with Ivan's. There was a hunger in his eyes, which glowed a deep amber as he stared at the tiara.

"It's mine," he said simply.

And Belle believed him.

14

RIFT

"Ivan." Rift grabbed his brother's other arm and held him tight even as he tried to pull away.

It's like he's possessed, Rift's snow leopard said.

Maybe he is. Rift followed his brother's gaze which was fixed on a piece of jewelry Rosie had given to her mom.

Why would Ivan want that? His snow leopard huffed. Whatever that is.

"Where did you find that?" Ivan's blunt tone was completely out of character. Even if someone messed up in the kitchen or dropped a dish he'd spent hours making, he always kept his calm.

There's something wrong with him, Rift's snow leopard's worry was evident in his tone.

"My daughter found it in the backyard of the house my uncle was staying in for the last couple of months," Belle explained quickly.

"Belle's uncle is Reginald." Rift loosened his grip on Ivan a little. "The location spell led us to her. The toy Oscar found in the evidence was hers." He sucked in a breath. "Murray was Belle's father."

"Murray?" Valerie covered her mouth with her hand. "You are the daughter of the man who kidnapped my sons?"

Katrina stood up, placing herself between her daughter and the rest of the people in the restaurant. "We weren't together when he..." Katrina couldn't bring herself to say the words.

"They had nothing to do with it," Aiden confirmed. "Caleb and I believe that completely."

Valerie reached for the back of her chair and sat down heavily. "I'm sorry, I'm protective of my sons."

"And I'm protective of my daughter. And my grandchildren." Katrina relaxed her shoulders. "Maybe we should sit down and discuss this calmly."

"Can I hold it?" Ivan seemed oblivious to everything but the tiara.

"Of course." Katrina handed it over without hesitation.

Stretching across the table, Rift took the tiara from his mate and then handed it to Ivan. "I've never seen it before. How come you know what it is?"

"It sings to me," Ivan replied, his hand shaking as he touched the jewels for the first time. "It's like it's a part of me."

"Mom?" Caleb went to Valerie who had gone deathly pale.

"I think..." She cleared her throat. "I think it's part of Ivan's treasure."

"Ivan has treasure?" Flora's shock matched everyone else's in the room.

"He does," Valerie confirmed. "At least, his parents would probably have had treasure but when Ivan came to me, he had nothing. All dragons do."

"Dragons? Those guys mentioned dragons…" Belle's eyes went wide, and she looked to Rift for answers.

"Ivan is a dragon shifter," Rift explained.

"Of course he is." She placed her hands, palms down, on

the table and leaned forward as if she'd gone weak at the knees.

We should go to her, his snow leopard said.

Not now. We need to stay with Ivan. He's behaving a little unpredictably right now.

Their unpredictable brother was holding the tiara cupped in his hands, stroking it repeatedly as if it were a pet cat. His eyes glowed a deep amber as he stared at the tiara. It was as if he was hypnotized by it.

"What's a dragon shifter?" Jack asked.

"Oh..." Belle dragged her gaze from Ivan who she'd been watching with some suspicion and switched it to her son. "We should talk about this later."

"Why don't we all sit down and eat?" Elise got up from her seat and went to Ivan. "Come on, we should go get the rest of the food from the kitchen. Caleb will be eating the tables if he doesn't eat soon."

Elise slid her arm around Ivan's shoulders and guided him out of the restaurant, which was filled with shocked silence. Questions would come later, but right now they were all trying to process what had happened. Particularly Ivan.

"Go," Belle waved him away when he hesitated, torn between his mate who was visibly upset, and his brother who was in a deep state of shock.

More of a deep state of bewilderment, his snow leopard remarked. It's like the tiara has put a spell on him.

"I'll go get the rest of the food," Caleb said and followed them out.

"Ivan," Elise said gently. "Are you okay?"

They made it to the kitchen, Ivan still cradled the tiara in his hands as if it were a small animal in need of protection. He blinked unseeing as he looked at Elise, but then the amber glow in his eyes subsided and color returned to his cheeks.

"Does everyone like the food?" Ivan asked.

"Yeah." Rift ran his hand through his hair as Caleb grabbed the rest of the plates and headed back out into the restaurant.

As soon as he'd gone out, Valerie came into the kitchen. "What happened today?" she demanded.

"We used the location spell. It led us to Belle and her family." Rift swallowed, unsure as to whether he should tell the rest of the story in front of Ivan.

He might get agitated if he hears someone is after his treasure. I've never seen him so possessive. I mean I thought he was bad enough over his pans, but this is something else, Rift's snow leopard said.

"And you're sure she is your mate?" Valerie asked sharply.

Rift took a step back from his mother. "Absolutely."

"Elise, do you know of a spell or some fae fruit or herb Rift might have consumed to make him think Belle is his mate?" Valerie's eyes bored into Elise.

Her brows furrowed together as she instantly shook her head. "No. And I was there, this isn't some kind of magic. I'm certain of it."

"There's a lot in this world we can be certain of, and a lot we must question." Valerie glanced at the tiara in Ivan's hands as if it were a bomb about to detonate.

"What do you know about my treasure?" Ivan moved closer to Valerie. "I always thought I didn't have any."

"You don't." The color in her cheeks heightened. "At least...you would have had some. All dragons have treasure. But whatever happened to it, no one knows."

"Who are my parents?" Ivan asked.

Valerie's face crumpled and she covered her mouth with her hand as she shook her head. "I don't know. You were given to me to raise because you were an orphan who needed a home. The dragons from across the water wanted to raise you there. But they eventually agreed that you could stay here with me."

"Why did they agree?" Ivan asked. "From what I've been told about the dragons, they aren't known for their generous nature. Something must have swayed them."

"Someone interceded. It's true but I was never told the details." She switched her attention to Rift. "What else?"

"Is that it?" Ivan asked.

"You know as much as I do." Valerie glanced at her son but didn't hold his gaze. "And I don't think it's worth dwelling on it right now. That came from outside of Wishing Moon Bay. Which means the dragons are the least of our concerns." Valerie composed her features even though her eyes glistened with unshed tears.

"Mom is right," Rift agreed. "Belle didn't want anything to do with me. She asked me to leave, and we did. I had to respect her wishes."

"So how come she's here?" Valerie's eyes narrowed with suspicion.

"They were cleaning out Reginald's house. He was Katrina's brother, but she hadn't had any contact with him for years. The authorities contacted her since she is Reginald's next of kin. Today was supposed to be the day they finally drew a line under that part of their family history."

"So you left them at the house. Then what?" Valerie went to the coffee pot and Elise grabbed four cups and set them down on the counter.

As she poured the coffee, Rift checked out Ivan, before continuing, "We stopped for food. I went for a run to clear my head. When I got back, we got a call from Katrina. They were being followed by a truck and they asked us to go and help them."

"And you saw this truck?" Valerie asked.

I've never seen her so suspicious, his snow leopard said. Even when we were kids and she thought we'd been in trouble, she's never been this suspicious, it's as if she doesn't want to believe Belle is innocent.

She's just trying to protect us all, Rift assured his other side.

"We doubled back," Elise picked up the story. "Katrina told us roughly where they were, and we drove to meet them. We swapped places. The children and Katrina got in the truck with Flora, while the rest of us went with Belle."

"We wanted to protect the children," Rift told her bluntly.

Valerie handed a cup of coffee to Rift. "I know this is tough, but it's important we make sure that what happened is real. You've lived in Wishing Moon Bay all your life. You know about magic. You know what happened with Sophie. Things are not always as they seem."

"Especially if it's something that you really want to see," Rift added.

"I know how you must feel about Belle. I'm trying to protect you as much as anyone else. I don't want you to lose your heart to an imposter," Valerie told him.

"She isn't an imposter," Rift replied.

"I believe Belle is innocent in all of this." Elise cupped her coffee in her hands and went to stand next to Rift. "We split up. We made sure Flora was safely away before we turned in the opposite direction, making sure the truck saw us. They followed us. We managed to plan an ambush and they fell for it."

"They were looking for something that they believed Reggie had. The treasure." Rift pointed at the tiara. "Only none of us knew anything about it."

"You believe the children when they say they found it in the backyard and that Belle or her mom had no idea about it?" Valerie seemed calmer now.

"You're the expert on children," Rift said drily. "Could they have lied so convincingly?"

"No." Valerie set her coffee cup down on the counter and came to Rift. She held out her arms, uncertainty in her eyes. "I'm sorry. I had to be certain. For all of our sake."

Rift sighed and nodded. "I understand." He hugged the woman who had raised him, the person who had given him a safe place to grow and learn about the world around him.

As a child and an adult, Rift has always known his mom would be there for him no matter what. Her questioning might have been harsh, but it was only because she loved her sons so much.

She is trying to protect us just like she always has, his snow leopard said.

But as he held her in his arms, Rift's eyes lingered on the tiara in Ivan's hand.

He had a feeling that Valerie might not be able to protect them from what was to come.

15

BELLE

"This is not exactly how I wanted to introduce you to my family." Rift watched the children as they ran around on the sand. He'd brought them here after they'd all eaten so that they could talk.

Katrina was back at the hotel resting in the spare room of Valerie's apartment. Belle was unsure if she was as tired as she'd made out or whether she thought Belle needed some time alone with Rift.

"I don't think either of us could have foreseen the kind of day we'd have today." Belle folded her arms across her body. Her mind was filled with a constant stream of thoughts that circled around and around like vultures over a dead body.

"You can say that again." Rift laughed lightly. "Part of me is just incredibly grateful I've met you at last, but part of me wonders if we hadn't come to the house, you wouldn't have told Jack and Rosie to play in the backyard..."

"And they wouldn't have found the tiara." She cocked her head on one side as she studied him. "I don't think that would have been better than this."

"You don't?" he asked warily.

"Those men would still have come after us. We wouldn't have given them what they wanted..." She shrugged, shying away from thinking about that outcome. "And anyway, we're here, it is what it is. I've learned that there's no point in what-ifs." She opened her arms. "This is where we are. This is what we have to deal with. So let's deal."

"That's one way to look at things."

"How is your brother? He seemed kind of freaked out when he saw the tiara." She looked down at the sand and dug her toe in the soft grains until it was half-buried before she asked, "Is he really a dragon shifter?"

"Yeah. He really is a dragon shifter." Rift stuffed his hands in his pockets and swung around to look out across the ocean. "The dragons live on an island someway off the coast. They rarely come here. We're inferior to them."

"Wow!" She lifted her head and stood shoulder to shoulder with him as they looked out at the horizon. "Inferior, huh?"

"Yeah." He lowered his gaze, watching Jack and Rosie as they knelt on the sand, scooping it into a mound that would no doubt be fashioned into a castle for a princess.

"Do you think Reggie knew where the rest of the treasure is hidden?" She didn't look at him. Had her uncle been responsible for the death of Ivan's parents and Aiden and Caleb's? What kind of monster was she related to?

"I have no idea," Rift confessed. "And I don't know how we'd find out."

"We could go through his stuff in the car," she offered. "And I suppose we could go back to the house and take a look around. We could dig up the backyard."

"I don't think we'd need to," Rift replied. "If Ivan went there, he would sense it, I'm sure. It's like a part of him. I've never seen him like that. I'm sorry if he frightened you and the children."

"Rosie is more upset about the tiara belonging to Ivan than anything else. He didn't scare her."

"But he scared you." Rift pressed his lips together as he looked down at her.

"He did. But I understand he overreacted, and I don't think he would have hurt anyone." She smiled as she nodded toward Rosie. "I have seen Rosie when Jack teases her by grabbing Jazzy and dangling her out of the window. It's not pretty."

"Jazzy?" Rift asked.

"The scrappy doll Rosie carries around with her. She's had her for as long as she can remember. It's like a part of her just like the tiara is a part of Ivan."

"We'll figure this all out," he assured her.

"Yeah. We will." She slipped her hand into the crook of his elbow. "I'm trusting fate brought us all together for a reason. And we are going to figure it all out and put things right."

"Put things right?" Rift looked down at her, a pink tinge in his cheeks as heat crept across his skin. He had a similar effect on her. The nearness of him, a simple touch, all set her heart racing and spread warmth through her body. Being near Rift was like being surrounded by a soft warm blanket.

He made her feel safe even though she was probably the least safe she'd ever been in her life.

"Yes. My family seems to have been responsible for a lot of misery. And I'd like to help set that right." She pulled him forward as the children stood up and trailed along the beach looking for shells to decorate their castle. "I don't want them to get too far away."

"Wishing Moon Bay is a safe place." Despite his words, he followed the children along the beach.

"I thought my world was safe until today." She shivered and leaned into him. "But hearing about my dad and what he did. It just reminds me that no one is ever really safe."

"Hey, why don't we go and make a wish?" Rift slipped his hand around hers and pulled her forward, running toward the children who were picking up shells and putting them in a pile next to their sandcastle.

"I don't believe wishes come true," she told him. "Children make them all the time. When they blow out their birthday candles, when they see a shooting star. They don't come true."

"These are special wishes," Rift assured her.

"All wishes are special. That doesn't mean they'll come true." She stopped walking and turned to face him. "I just don't want the kids to feel the same disappointment I did when I was a kid."

"I'm sorry you feel that way." Rift ran his thumb over the back of her hand. As warmth spread across her skin, her forehead creased. Perhaps she was wrong. Maybe wishes did come true but not in the ways she expected.

Hadn't she wished her children would have their dad back? When Jack hid his disappointment when his dad didn't come to watch his baseball game, she made the wish. Was Rift the dad her kids deserved, the dad they needed?

Perhaps wishes were better if they were not too specific, if they were left to fate to fulfill in whatever way it saw fit. Certainly, Landon was never going to win the best dad of the year award, he'd proved that often enough. But Rift, there was something about him. He was attentive and kind and obviously loved kids.

"You know if Rosie makes a wish now, it'll be to get to keep the tiara. And Jack will wish to stay here forever and not go to school." She glanced at Rift. "Neither of those is likely to come true, are they?"

"I believe anything is possible."

"The way Ivan looked at that tiara, there is no way he'll

ever give it up." They began walking again. "And that's okay, it's his and it's right that he keeps it."

Rift stared out across the ocean once more. "I hope he's going to be okay."

"He looked haunted. As if there was a part of him missing." She squeezed Rift's hand. "I'm sorry. We seem to have upset your family by coming here."

"None of this is your fault."

She chuckled. "That one is going to come back and haunt me forever."

Rift grinned. "I like the sound of forever."

"See, that would be your wish," her expression sobered. "And I don't know if that is something I can give you." She held out her hand to the ocean. "This is your home and it's beautiful. Your family needs you. But we have our lives elsewhere."

"I'd go wherever you go," he promised her, and she believed him.

"But would you be happy?" She watched the children run back to their sandcastle with handfuls of shells. "Because if you weren't then that would be my fault."

"I'll be happy wherever you are. The only way you'll ever make me miserable is if you send me away." He laughed and pulled her forward into a run. "No pressure or anything."

She laughed as they ran across the sand, stumbling as her feet caught in a clump of seaweed. But Rift kept her on her feet and made sure she didn't fall to her knees.

"Wow, this looks cool." Rift let go of Belle's hand and dropped to his knees next to the sandcastle, which the children had molded out of the pile of sand they'd heaped up. Jack had used a stick to shape the sand and carve out turrets. Now they were decorating the walls with the shells.

"Do you like it?" Jack's eyes shone as he looked up at Rift.

"We were going to build a moat and fill it with water, but we don't have anything to carry it with from the ocean."

"Next time we come we can bring a couple of buckets and build a wide moat." He dug out his phone and scrolled through his photos. "Here's one I built with Milo. He's my brother's son."

"You built that?" Jack was obviously impressed.

"Yes. Maybe we could bring Milo, too. He's about the same age as you." Rift sorted through the shells they'd collected but instead of picking up the delicate shells, he grabbed a small flat stone that had a golden sheen.

"That's so pretty, we were going to put it on the front of the castle," Rosie told him.

"This is a special stone. You should keep it." He held it in the palm of his hand.

"Why is it special?" Rosie closed her fingers around it and held it in her hand.

"It's a wish stone," Rift replied.

"A wish stone?" Belle knelt beside Rosie and ran her finger over the smooth surface of the stone.

"These stones are what makes the wishes of Wishing Moon Bay so special," Rift explained.

"Is that so?" Belle had to admit the stones did look pretty special.

Rift tilted his head to one side and studied her for a moment. Her lips twitched at the corners and she nodded almost imperceptibly. Despite what she'd said, she didn't want her kids to grow up without wishes, without hope. As she watched Rift with her kids, she realized that he gave her hope.

Despite everything that had happened and the danger they faced ahead, today had been a good day. Even with Ivan's disturbing reaction to the tiara, Belle honestly believed that Rift's family were good people. If she chose to, she could become part of that family.

Her wish would come true.

"It is a wish stone. When you find one, you hold it in your hand and close your eyes. Then you focus on your wish before throwing it into the ocean."

Jack jumped to his feet, all thoughts of decorating the castle gone as he whirled around and ran off toward the tide line. "I'm going to find a wish stone and make a wish."

"Come on, Mommy," Rosie held out her hand to Belle. "You need to find a wish stone, too."

"You're right, I do. Will you help me?" Belle got to her feet, and Rosie dragged her after Jack.

"I will," Rosie promised.

"Come on, Rift. You should help, too." Jack beckoned to the snow leopard shifter who sprang to his feet and jogged after them. "Are there any good places to look?"

"Yes, we should head a little farther along the beach. The ocean current often washes them up there. Come on." He held out his hand to Jack who was usually reserved with people he didn't know, particularly men. But he slid his hand into Rift's and ran alongside him, jumping back and forth along the tide line.

"You look happy, Mommy." Rosie's words pierced Belle's heart.

"I am happy, Rosie." She scooped her daughter up in her arms and kissed her cheek. "I love you."

"I love you, too." Rosie flung her arms around her neck and gave her a salty kiss. "And I love it here."

"Me, too." But this was a dream, like when you go to a beautiful place on vacation. A brief spell of time that couldn't last.

No matter how hard you wished, real life eventually came crashing back down.

16

RIFT

"Okay. Do you all have your wishing stones?" Rift glanced at Rosie and Jack who had taken off their socks and shoes and were standing up to their knees in the ocean. Belle was next to him, her stone in her hand and her cheeks flushed with color as her eyes sparkled like the sun on the ocean.

"Yes!" Jack and Rosie jumped up and down, soaking their clothes with salty seawater.

"Close your eyes and make your wish." Rift grasped his stone tightly and closed his eyes. There was only one wish he could make. Only one wish he needed to come true.

That these three people will stay in our lives forever, his snow leopard shared the same wish.

"Ready?" Rift asked.

"Ready." Jack turned his excited face to Rift. "Can we throw them?"

"Yes." Rift pulled his arm back and then launched his wish stone into the ocean where it landed with a satisfying plop.

The others did the same, with Jack straining to throw his as far as possible. "Look at that! It landed on that wave."

"How long until our wishes come true?" Rosie's high breathy voice filled with excitement mixed with the swish of the waves as they lapped over the sand.

"There's no set time," Rift told her. "They come true when the time is right."

"We have to be patient," Belle added. "Shall we go get an ice cream?" She glanced at Rift. "There is ice cream in Wishing Moon Bay, isn't there?"

He cracked a smile. "The best ice cream. And then we can go to my brother's store where they sell candies that make you croak like a frog."

"They don't," Belle's tone showed her uncertainty. She was still trying to figure out the town and its inhabitants.

Maybe once she eats a candy and croaks like a frog, she might find it easier to believe in wishes coming true, Rift's snow leopard said.

There's nothing more magical than croaking like a frog, Rift agreed.

"They do," Rift confirmed. "Two of my brothers opened the store along with their mates, who are also sisters."

"Your family is filled with coincidences." Belle brushed the sand from her hands. "Okay, ice cream and then croaking candies. I know I'm going to regret it since it'll be a sugar overload for you guys."

"Come on, Rosie. Let's go." Jack skipped out of the ocean, splashing in the waves as he ran.

"Do you have strawberry ice cream here?" Rosie slid her hand into Rift's as they strolled back to the parking lot.

"They do. I like strawberry and white chocolate ice cream. Have you ever tried that flavor?" he asked.

"No. It sounds yummy." She licked her lips as her feet dragged through the sand. "Can you carry me?" Rosie held up her arms and Rift checked with Belle before he picked her up, cradling her against his chest. "It's been a fun day but I'm tired."

"It has been a fun day." Belle linked her arm through his and they continued up the beach. He could almost imagine that this was his wife, these were his children and they lived here in town. Happily. He glanced over his shoulder at the ocean, if only his wish would come true.

If only this was his reality.

If only we could figure out how to deal with the men who want Ivan's treasure, his snow leopard said.

That's next on the list after ice cream and croaking candy, he assured his other side. There's no way for us to move on and make decisions if that's left unresolved.

I'll miss this place if we leave, his snow leopard sighed.

Me, too. His arm tightened around Rosie. But we have so much to gain. Our lives will never be fulfilled if we live here without our mate and her family.

They reached the parking lot where Belle had parked her car. Reggie's stuff was still in the trunk. Belle and Katrina planned to go through it later after the children had gone to bed. After making sure the children were securely in their seats, Belle drove along the coast to an ice cream parlor where they enjoyed their ice cream while staring out at the ocean.

When they reached the candy store, they were all relaxed and happy as if nothing had ever happened. Nothing bad at least.

"Hi, there!" Penny rushed to meet them as Rift entered the store, with the others behind him.

"Hi, Penny. How are you doing?" Rift hugged her gently. "Your baby is getting big."

"Don't I know it." Penny ran her hand over her swollen belly. "It's getting harder to keep on the go all day. When I had Milo, it was easier, I could sit down and put my feet up when I got tired. Not so easy when I have an excitable son who wants to explore everything."

"I thought Milo might like to meet Jack and Rosie." Rift stepped to the side and the children and Belle gathered around him.

"He'd love to meet you." Penny smiled warmly, her hand absently stroking her baby bump. "We're newish in town, so he needs to make new friends. Maybe we could arrange a playdate?"

"Oh, this is Belle, their mom." Rift rolled his eyes. "I'm not good at this."

"You're doing fine," Penny assured him. "Hi, I'm Penny. Good to meet you, Belle. It's great to have another woman to even things out in the family."

"I'm not..." Belle started but then grinned. "I'm not good at this either. It's good to meet you." She ran her hand over Jack's head. "We were told that you have some croaking candies."

"We do!" Penny beckoned them forward. "Come on, you can try them. Milo thinks they are hysterical."

"They make you croak?" Jack asked.

"They do." Penny took a jar off the shelf and unscrewed the lid. "Here, try one."

"Will it hurt?" Rosie picked out a sweet and held it an inch from her mouth.

"No, they don't hurt. They are made from candy, but we sprinkle a little bit of magic into each one so that you croak like a frog." She offered the jar to Rift. "Here, Rift can show you."

"I can." He frowned and then laughed as he took a piece of frog-shaped green candy, complete with small bumps that looked like eyes, and popped it in his mouth. "Tastes nice."

"Not like frog slime?" Jack wrinkled his nose and stuck out his tongue to lick the green candy.

"Not like..." His words dried up and instead he croaked like a frog. His eyes went wide, and the children and Belle collapsed into fits of giggles. He croaked again. There was no way to form words. It was as if his mouth was malfunctioning.

"Let me try!" Jack popped the candy in his mouth, and Rosie did the same.

"I like this," Belle chuckled as her children croaked and hopped around the store. "They can't answer me back when I ask them to do something."

"Oh, that's a great idea!" Penny said. "We could make shut-up sweets, I could give one to Logan when he acts like I'm sick instead of pregnant." She tapped her chin thoughtfully. "Although, I might regret that since he often offers to do the dishes so that I can go rest in the evening. I do like curling up with a good book for half an hour while he cleans the kitchen."

"When are you due?" Belle asked as Rift and the children croaked at each other.

"Not for another three months. I'm enjoying every minute of it." She stroked her baby bump once more. "It seems more special this time around. I guess it's because I know that Logan wants this baby so much." She glanced at Rift. "There's something to be said for a shifter mate. Even if they are a little childish."

Rift opened his mouth and croaked the longest croak that had ever been croaked. Jack immediately copied him while Rosie made a croaking song.

Penny is right, you are childish, his snow leopard said.

That's because we have waited for children for so long. And now they were here. They might not be his flesh and blood, but they were a part of him, and he would always be there for them.

As he watched Penny and Belle talk, he couldn't help

wishing that he might one day be lucky enough to have a child of his own. He'd love to watch Belle's belly swell, to feel the child inside of her kicking and moving around.

But if it didn't happen, he'd be okay. Jack and Rosie were wonderful, and he planned to show them the world.

Our world, his snow leopard said. The world we grew up in.

Yet there was still that nagging thought that they might have to leave their home. But wherever they were, wherever they lived, there was a world to explore.

"Okay. Are you going to choose some candy?" Belle asked. "We need to get back to the hotel so I can unload the boxes from the trunk. And you both need some downtime."

"Choose whatever you want. It's on the house," Penny told the children.

"Are you sure?" Belle asked. "I have money."

"I'm sure. You're family." Penny grinned and touched Rift's arm as she passed him.

"Thanks, Penny." He couldn't remember not having his brother's mates in his life even though they hadn't been together for too long.

Just as he could no longer imagine not having Belle in his life.

But it was time to face reality. Time to unpack the boxes from the car and try to figure out what exactly was going on and how Murray and Reggie were linked to Ivan.

17

BELLE

"I don't see anything in this stuff that helps us." Belle stood with her hands on her hips surveying the items they'd boxed up from Reggie's house. For the last hour or more, they had sifted through it, separating it into piles. Books, clothes, paperwork, including invoices and receipts for everything from gas to toilet paper.

"I agree." Katrina straightened her back and stretched her hands over her head but didn't get up from the floor where she sat on a cushion, leaning against the wall. Valerie had given them the use of one of the hotel storerooms.

"Look, I need to get the children into bed. Rift has been watching them for the last couple of hours and I'm sure he needs a break." She stifled a yawn as she headed for the door.

"We're going to leave it like this?" Katrina asked.

"Yes. I want to come back and take another look tomorrow with fresh eyes. Maybe we've missed something but right now I'm too tired to see straight." She held out her hand for her mom. "Valerie gave us a key. No one is coming in here. It'll be exactly the same in the morning."

"You're right, I was just hoping that we would find something today." Katrina's eyes misted with tears as she stared at the neat piles of Reggie's belongings. "I want this over. I want to put Reggie behind me. I can't believe it. It's like he's haunting us from beyond the grave."

"He's not haunting us, and we will figure it out. Rift said their detective friend will come over first thing tomorrow. Maybe he might see something here that we missed." Belle slid her arm around her mom's shoulders and hugged her close. "We're lucky there are so many people here that want to help us. We're not alone."

Katrina hiccupped and a sob erupted from deep within her, leaving her trembling in her daughter's arms. "After I moved away because of your father, I was alone. I always felt as if it was a curse I passed on to you. When Landon left you, it was as if I'd tainted you in some way."

"You know that's not true. You are not responsible for any of this. Life happens. You can't control how other people behave."

"But I knew what Reggie was into. I should have steered away from Murray." Katrina slipped out of her daughter's arms, miserable and haunted by the past.

"And then I would never have been born. And neither would Jack or Rosie." Belle shrugged. "Let go of any regrets you have, Mom. Maybe it's time for us to both move on and begin to trust others around us. And believe that they are good and won't disappear on us. Okay?"

"Okay." Katrina wiped her hands over her face and sniffed loudly. "When I see you with Rift, when I watch him with the children, I can believe that things will change."

Belle swallowed hard, her emotions were simmering just under the surface, ready to erupt and she didn't want to cry. She didn't want to go back to the hotel room with red-rimmed eyes. "I think I could love him."

"Of course you can love him," Katrina said fiercely. "Open your heart to him."

"My heart is open," Belle replied. "I mean I think I could already be a little bit in love with him." Her brows knitted together. "And that scares me. I don't want to make a mistake. Not when I have the children to think about."

"There's no mistake. And the children deserve a man like him to call their dad." Katrina scooped her daughter up in her arms. "Take a breath. Accept your fate."

Belle laughed and wiped her eyes before her tears fell. "Fate. What the hell is that all about?"

"Maybe we shouldn't question it. Maybe we should just accept it as it is." Katrina pushed Belle away from her and placed her hands on her upper arms. As she looked into Belle's eyes, she said, "Seeing you together makes me happy. Even with all the rest of this crap going on, I can see a glimpse of the future and it's a good future."

"If...if I decide to stay here..."

Katrina's eyes widened and an equally wide smile spread across her lips. "You're thinking of moving here to Wishing Moon Bay?"

"I'm thinking this would be a wonderful place for the children to grow up. The beach and the ocean are amazing and the mountains... Jack would love it." She pressed her lips together. "Do you think I'm crazy?"

"No, I think for the first time in a long time you are making choices that are right for you and the children. That you've found the courage to make changes in your lives for the better." Katrina nodded.

"If we do, would you move here, too?" Belle couldn't imagine not having her mom around. She also hated the idea of her mom being far away and on her own. It had been the two of them against the world for so long. Too long.

How would Katrina live alone against the world?

"Don't you think it's time you cut the apron strings and lived away from your mom?" Katrina asked. "You'd have a man in your life, a good man. You don't want me around cramping your style."

"Firstly, I have no style," Belle laughed. "And secondly, I love you. The kids love you, and I don't know how we'd have coped without you these last few months. And Rift is all about family. He would want you to be here."

Katrina tilted her head to one side and arched an eyebrow. "So you already know how that man of yours thinks."

Belle chuckled. "A little. He's pretty transparent where family is concerned."

"I'll think about it." Katrina linked arms with Belle as she opened the storeroom door and went out into the cool corridor. "But I want you to think about it, too. Make sure it's what you want." Her eyes lingered on the boxes before Belle switched off the light. "I don't want me to be a constant reminder of the past. Not when you have such an amazing future to look forward to with Rift."

"My past is part of who I am," Belle replied as she locked the door and pocketed the key. "I don't think it's a good idea to completely forget who you are. A little part of me wants to remember how miserable I've been so that I can genuinely appreciate how happy I am."

"I love you, Belle. And I'm incredibly proud of you." Katrina hugged her again.

"I love you, too, Mom. It's because of you that I'm who I am." She sucked in a deep breath. "Look at us."

"It's been an emotional day." Katrina wiped her eyes and then turned away from the storeroom and headed along the corridor.

"Once the children are in bed, I might go out for some fresh air. I need to clear my head. If you don't mind." They reached the reception area. Jeremy, the receptionist, gave them a curious look and Belle lifted her hand and waved to him.

He nodded to her. "Good evening."

"Evening, Jeremy." Belle smiled, wanting him to like her. She wanted all the people here to like her. Would she find a way to fit into Rift's life?

"Hi there, Jeremy." Katrina lifted her hand and gave him a brief wave, which he returned with a smile and then went back to work.

"I love the hotel." Belle looked up at the ornate ceiling as they walked upstairs. "It's so quirky."

"Do you wonder how many secrets this place must hold? It's so old, there must have been some scandalous behavior by the guests." Katrina stopped halfway up the stairs and turned around to look at the reception area below. "If we do move here, I might ask Valerie if there are any vacancies."

"You'd work in the hotel?" Belle asked, pleased her mom was making plans about their possible move here.

"I'd need a job. I don't want to take on anything too stressful. I think working here would be a good way to meet people and become part of the town." Katrina turned around and they continued up the stairs. "What about you?"

"I have no idea," Belle confessed. She currently worked as a PA at an investment firm. Did they have such things in Wishing Moon Bay? "I'd like to explore the town some more and maybe talk to Rift about it. Although, I don't want him getting his hopes up."

"I think his hopes should be up." Katrina nudged her daughter gently. "I think you have already made up your mind about moving here."

"I haven't." Belle still had doubts. She didn't want her decision to be a knee-jerk reaction because of the events of today. "I'm not making any decision until we figure out how to deal with those guys. This has to be a decision we make based on what we want, not based on fear of what might happen if we go back to our old lives."

"This is what you want, Belle. I see it in your eyes."

Belle sighed and ran her fingers through her hair. She needed a shower and bed, but her mind was racing around and around in circles and she needed to quieten it if she was ever going to get some sleep. "This is what I think I want. But am I just clutching hold of the dream I had of what family life would be like? Am I trying to insert Rift into the role of father to the kids even though I don't really know him?"

"Then get to know him." Katrina stopped outside their hotel room door. "Why don't I put the children to bed while you go for a walk with Rift?"

"No, I can put them to bed." Belle stared at the door as if she could see behind it, the temptation to take up her mother's offer was strong.

"Do it. Spend time with him. We have no idea where tomorrow will take us, so why not get to know him a little better." Katrina opened the hotel room door before Belle had a chance to answer.

As they went inside, the sound of giggling filled the room. Rift was playing a board game with the children who seemed happy and relaxed. The scene made Belle's heart squeeze and her eyes smarted as she blinked away her tears.

"Mommy! I'm winning," Rosie declared when she saw them.

"You are?" Belle knelt beside her daughter and kissed the top of her head.

"I am." She nodded. "Rift found the game in the attic, he used to play it with his brothers when he was young."

"The attic is filled with stuff from when we were kids," Rift told her. "Valerie is not good at getting rid of things. I think she kept them all this time hoping that her grandchildren would play with them. She's had to wait a long time."

"I'm the same," Belle confessed. "It's hard to part with things when the kids grow out of them. My attic will be full to bursting by the time the children are grown up."

"Can we see all the things you've kept?" Rosie's eyes sparkled with excitement.

"When we have time," Belle confirmed. "But, right now, you should get to bed."

"We haven't finished our game." But Jack yawned all the same.

"We can finish it tomorrow," Rift promised. "You've had a long day. You don't want to be tired in the morning."

"Oh!" Rosie clapped her hands together excitedly and got up from the floor where she'd been sitting beside the game board which was on a small table that hadn't been in the room earlier. "Can we go play with Milo tomorrow morning? His Mom called Rift and asked us to go to their house. Can we?"

"I hope you don't mind," Rift began. "Valerie told Penny that Oscar was coming over and she thought it would be easier for you."

"It would be easier," Belle agreed. "They don't need to listen to us grown-ups talk."

"So, can we go?" Rosie asked hopefully.

"You can." Belle glanced at Jack. "If you want to."

"I do." Jack got up slowly from the floor. "I just wish I had some of my toys here. And some other clothes." He looked down at the clothes he was wearing. "We don't have any of our stuff."

"Valerie can help there, too," Rift replied. "She dug out some clothes for you to wear. Luckily, jeans and T-shirts never go out of date. And she found some overalls that should fit Rosie." Rift stood up and stepped toward the door.

"Which reminds me, she said she'd put them through the washer. They should be dry by now. She also found some pajamas, too."

"It sounds as if Valerie is worse than me for keeping stuff," Belle joked.

"You have no idea." He pulled open the door and stepped out into the corridor. "I'll be back in a flash."

"Okay, kids, let's start getting our teeth brushed and our faces washed. Your Mom is going to go out for some fresh air, so you've got me to put you to bed and read you a story." Katrina held out her hands. "Is that okay?"

"Yes! I love your stories," Rosie ran to the adjoining bathroom.

"I'm beginning to feel a little obsolete," Belle joked. "Rift is good at entertaining and you are great at bedtime stories..."

"But you have the best hugs, Mom," Jack told her as he jumped into her arms.

"And that is my most favorite thing." Belle kissed his cheek and held him tightly.

A sense of peace and happiness settled on her. She was exactly where she was supposed to be.

Things would work out, she could feel it in her bones.

18

RIFT

"Are you busy?" Belle met him at the door when he returned with the pajamas that Valerie had washed, dried, and pressed. The smell reminded him of his childhood, a happy childhood. He hoped he could one day recreate moments of that childhood for Jack and Rosie.

"Not really." He'd planned to go for a run in the mountains to let off steam and clear his head. He needed to be prepared for tomorrow's meeting with Oscar where they would make a plan on how to deal with the threat to Belle and her family. "Is there something you need?"

He'd be more than willing to get anything Belle wanted or needed. No matter how far he had to travel or what it cost.

Have you listened to yourself? His snow leopard chuckled to himself.

And you wouldn't do the same if she asked you for something? Rift retorted.

True. His snow leopard settled down and rested his head on his large paws. Maybe she wants to see me. Maybe she wants you to shift so she can spend time with me. Would you do that if it's what

Belle wanted? His snow leopard arched his eyebrow, as if he had an eyebrow.

You know I would. Belle is our *mate. Not mine. Not yours.* Rift knew his other side was teasing him. There was no jealousy between them even where time spent with their mate was concerned.

"I wanted to get some fresh air. My head is filled with so much stuff going around and around like a tornado." She twisted her hands together and looked down at the floor. "You probably have stuff to do. And you've already given us so much of your time. Thanks for looking after the children."

"No problem at all." He held out the pajamas to his mate. "I can wait while you put the children to bed."

"Oh, Mom said she'd do it." Belle rolled her eyes with an amused smile. "And they've already made it clear that they enjoy her bedtime stories more than mine."

Rift smothered a smile. "They don't mean it."

"Oh, they probably do. I suppose I tend to rush things sometimes. There's always a pile of dishes or laundry waiting for me after they've gone to bed. The perks of being a single working parent." Her mouth curled up at one corner and he itched to lean forward and kiss her.

"I know how hard it was for Valerie. And Penny, too." He took a step back. "I'll be loitering in the corridor. Take your time."

"Thanks." She lingered in the doorway for a moment before she backed away and closed the door.

He leaned against the wall, looking up at the ceiling. He'd wait forever for her. But he sensed Belle returning almost immediately.

Straightening up, he brushed his hands down the front of his shirt. If he'd known he was going for a walk with Belle, he'd have gotten changed when he went to get the pajamas.

Luckily, he'd had a chance to shower in Valerie's apartment earlier.

She didn't ask you for a walk so she can smell your armpits, his snow leopard told him bluntly.

Rift ignored the taunt as he led Belle down the stairs and into the reception area. Jeremy was behind the desk, watching everything from under his lashes as usual. The guy might have been a pain in the ass when he first arrived at the hotel, but he was good at his job and conscientious, if a little too nosy. Nothing passed the guy by.

Something we might be thankful for one day, his snow leopard remarked.

"So, where do you want to go?" Rift asked.

"I don't know. We could walk the grounds of the hotel. Or do you have a suggestion?" They exited the hotel and Belle stopped on the steps, her mouth hanging open as she stared at the full moon hanging in the sky above the bay. "Wow."

"I forget how beautiful it is." Rift stood by his mate's side and stared at the moon. It had never been so full or so bright. Or maybe it was the effect of having his mate by his side. Everything seemed bigger and brighter, colors more vivid, smells more potent.

"Can we go to the beach?" She didn't take her eyes off the moon. "I'd love to lie on the sand and stare at the moon." She lifted her hand. "I feel as if I could reach out and touch it."

"Yes. We could find another wish stone. Wishes are more potent when made under the full moon." He held out his hand and she entwined her fingers with his as they ran down the steps and across the parking lot.

Belle fished her car keys out of her purse and unlocked the car. She took one last look at the moon before she slid into the driver's seat and started the engine. Rift darted round to the other side and climbed in.

"How is Ivan?" Belle drove out of the parking lot and

headed toward the beach. She didn't ask for directions and Rift wasn't sure if she remembered the way or if she was simply pointing the car in the direction of the moon.

"He's okay. He managed to get through dinner with the help of Elise. She said he's a little shell-shocked but he's better than he was. This has come as a shock to him." Rift side-eyed Belle. "And you? How are you, Belle?"

"I'm okay, I guess. I don't know if it's truly sunk in yet. You know, the danger we're in. Coming here to Wishing Moon Bay has left me feeling as if it was all a dream. It's as if I've become detached from my other life." She shrugged. "Does that make sense?"

"It does. And it's probably helped. You've had something else to focus on. Tomorrow, when we meet with Oscar, you'll be able to see things clearer."

"Because I haven't spent the day running around like a headless chicken in panic mode?" She gave a short laugh. "You're right. I don't know what we'd have done if we'd gone home instead of coming here."

"Katrina said they went to her house. Do you recall anyone suspicious visiting you? Maybe they didn't ask about Reggie, but maybe they were checking out where you live." Rift clenched his fists. His temper flared at the idea of anyone intending harm to Belle or her family.

Belle's not the only one who needs fresh air to clear their head, his snow leopard said. *Let go of it for tonight. It'll all still be there in the morning.*

You're right, Belle wanted to clear her head. All I'm doing is filling it with troubling thoughts.

"I don't remember anyone like that." Her forehead creased and her hands tightened around the steering wheel. "Maybe I missed something. But most of the time I'm so busy, I don't have time to think."

"So this is like a mini-vacation," Rift said lightly.

She grinned and nodded. "Yes, it is. I get to stay in a hotel and be served delicious food. There's also a great babysitter who my children adore." Color crept across her cheeks as she glanced sideways at him.

"I adore them, too. You have two wonderful children."

"Thanks. I always worried when their dad left that I might fail them. I was terrified of letting them down. At first, the responsibility was crushing but my mom was there for me." She took a breath. "I reminded myself that I turned out okay even though I was raised by a single mom."

"You turned out more than okay." He rubbed his hand over his chin and chuckled. "That was a cheesy line."

"I liked it." She slowed the car and stopped in the parking lot next to the beach. "Can I be honest with you, Rift?"

"I hope so."

She switched off the engine and put the keys in her purse. "I don't want anything complicated. If we're going to have a relationship, I want everything laid out in the open. I need honesty and trust."

"That's what you'll get from me. I promise." He reached out and covered her hand with his. "We're not young and naive, Belle. You have your kids, and I am happy to fit in around that. Whatever that means."

"I don't want you to sacrifice your happiness just to make us happy. This has to be a two-way relationship." She lifted her thumb and rubbed it over his fingers, sending a shock of electricity coursing through him. "If you'd told me a week ago that I'd be contemplating making a life with a man I've just met, I'd have told you that you were crazy. Honestly, after the breakdown of my marriage, I had sworn off men at least until the children were older."

"But then you met me." He winked at her. "Modesty is a natural trait of mine."

"You're right, then I met you. And then with what followed." She stared out at the moon high above. "This...our relationship seems like the only sane thing in the world right now."

"Belle, we'll figure the rest out." He leaned across the car and kissed her cheek, his lips soft on her skin as he inhaled her scent.

"I know we will. And then we'll figure the rest of it out." Her eyes shone with tears as she turned to face him, her eyes lingering on his lips. "Can we just kiss now and get it over with?"

He let out a short laugh. "Well, if you put it like that..."

She half-turned in her seat to face him and cupped his cheek with her hand. "I'm going to struggle to look at the moon when all I want to do is stare at your lips. And the only wish I can think of right now is for you to kiss me."

Her bottom lip trembled as she lowered her eyes. She seemed so lost and vulnerable in that moment. Rift covered her hand with his and leaned forward, his eyes fixed on her lips as he closed the space between them.

Belle sighed and ran her tongue along her bottom lip, inviting him to taste her mouth. How could he refuse?

Rift steeled himself, fighting for control as their lips met. A frisson of excitement raced up his spine and he wound his arm around her waist, pulling her closer to him, wishing they weren't trapped in the confines of the car.

He wanted to pick her up and carry her to the beach where he'd lay her on a blanket and make love to her beneath the full moon.

His lips moved against hers and she placed her hand on his chest, resting it lightly over his heart. Could she feel it thumping? Did she know it beat only for her now that they'd met?

Belle ran her tongue along his lower lip and opened her

mouth. He tasted her, her sweetness lingering on his tongue as their kiss broke.

"I can't remember the last time I made out in a car." She leaned her head on his shoulder, hiding her face from him.

"I'm here for you anytime you want to make out." He kissed her neck, nuzzling her soft skin.

"We should go look at the moon and make a wish." She didn't move. It was as if they were caught in a spell neither of them wanted to break.

"I don't think I have any wishes left to make," he murmured against her ear. "I have everything I want right here."

"Me, too." Her fingers curled around his neck and she lifted her head. "Everything I didn't know I wanted."

He smiled and stroked her cheek. "You are everything I know I wanted. And more."

19

BELLE

"It's almost as bright as day." Belle plonked herself down on the sand and lay back, not caring that she'd get sand in her hair. This was one of those moments she'd remember for the rest of her life.

"I used to come and lie under the full moon when I was younger. I'd question what my life was supposed to be. When I was going to meet my mate. And all the other stuff that seems so important when you're young." He sat down next to her and lay back, his fingers touching hers as they stared at the moon.

"I used to dream about what my life would be like," she confessed. "When I was growing up, I used to want to be an artist. I loved to paint." As she stared up at the moon, with all its imperfections, she wished she had a canvas and paints. But she hadn't painted for years. She'd never do it justice.

"What stopped you?" Rift asked.

"My mom worked so hard to raise me alone. As a teenager, I saw that and so I got a part-time job to help out and that led to me realizing that I needed to earn a good, regular wage. I went to college and became a PA." She turned her head to face him. "And I'm good at it. Even if I do say so myself."

"Do you enjoy it?"

"I do. I get a great deal of satisfaction from making sure things run smoothly." The prospect of giving up her job hit her in the stomach as if someone had punched her. Was she ready to give up everything she'd worked for?

"Have you ever thought of going into the hotel business?" Rift propped himself up on one elbow and stared at her. Which she found totally disarming.

"The hotel business? You mean your hotel?" Her heart rate increased, and a surge of excitement coursed through her. Then she tempered her excitement. "Are you making up a job for me so that I'll stay?"

"No." He stroked her cheek, and she shivered, her eyes drawn to his lips. However, she wanted to hear what he had to say and dragged her eyes back to the moon above them. "Valerie isn't getting any younger and the operation on her leg, although a success, it isn't getting stronger... She's going to need help soon."

"What about Ivan?"

"Ivan runs the kitchen, there's no way he'd take on the day-to-day running of the hotel. Logan and Dario have the candy store, and their mates are both expecting babies." He chuckled. "And Logan has tried running the hotel when Valerie was recuperating. He can do it, and he could do it, but he doesn't enjoy it. At all."

"If it's what Valerie wanted and I wasn't pushing anyone out, then I would consider it," she replied tactfully.

"Does that mean you would move here to Wishing Moon Bay?" Rift held his breath and so did she. This was a momentous decision. One she should give more thought to.

"Yes. The children love it here. I don't think Jack would ever forgive me if I gave up the opportunity to live in a place like this." She sucked in a deep breath. "It's scary, that's all. The thought of giving up everything we know, my job, the house, the kids' schools. I think it's scarier than those guys that are after us."

"We'd all be here for you. And Katrina." He took hold of her hand and ran his thumb across her skin. "She'd come with you, wouldn't she?"

"I asked her," Belle admitted. "Yes, we have already had this conversation. She said she would. I think it would be a good choice for all of us. A fresh start."

"Then my wishes truly have come true." He lay back and stared at the moon.

"Lying here, it all seems so simple." She sat up and brushed the sand off her hands. "Come on, you said we could find a wish stone and that the wishes are more potent if they're under the full moon."

"I did." He got up and leaned down, offering her his hand. "Does this mean you do believe in wishes now, too?"

"If I'm going to live in a town called Wishing Moon Bay, it's only right I believe. And since you are proof that dreams can come true, then I'm willing to be a believer."

She only had one wish as they searched the shoreline for a gold-colored stone. As exciting as it was to talk about their future together, none of it could happen unless she dealt with the specter of the past that hung over them. She didn't want to move to Wishing Moon Bay because they were in hiding. She wanted it to be a choice.

It could never be a choice unless they solved the mystery of Reggie's and Murray's involvement with the dragon treasure.

"Here's one." Rift pointed to a half-buried wish stone that had been brought in on the tide.

"Are you sure you don't want it?"

"I told you all my wishes had come true."

She picked it up, holding it in the palm of her hand as she went to the ocean and washed it off in the waves that gently lapped the shore. Then she held it out with her palm open, so the moon's rays shone down on it. When it was dry, she clutched it tightly in her palm and closed her eyes.

With her wish fully formed in her head, she opened her eyes and threw the stone into the ocean. As it disappeared beneath the waves, Rift stood behind her with his arms wrapped around her waist. She leaned back against him, the heat of his body warming her as the night grew chill.

He kissed her neck and she shivered in anticipation as he stroked the underside of her breasts.

She closed her eyes, reveling in his touch, wanting more. Perhaps they could find a place a little more private where they could spend some time alone. As she opened her eyes, something flew across the moon and she stiffened.

"What was that?" She pointed at the shape although it was harder to keep track of it as it flew across the sky.

"I don't know." Rift's arms dropped to his sides as he tracked the flying thing. Perhaps his senses would help him figure out what it was.

"Is it a big bird? A shifter bird?" Belle followed the direction of Rift's eyes, but she could only make out an occasional blurry movement. "Do shifter birds normally fly at night?"

"They can and they do, but I've never seen a bird that big." His forehead creased as he swiveled around. "I've lost sight of it."

"Was it your brother?" Had she just seen her first dragon shifter?

"No. He's at the hotel." Rift checked his watch. "Unless he's left Elise in charge of the kitchen."

"Are you okay?" Belle turned to face him, his skin looked pale, but maybe it was only because of the moonlight shining down on him.

"Yeah." He nodded but she wasn't convinced.

"Was it a dragon?" She could barely breathe, it was as if she were under the water, the weight of the ocean pressing down on her. "I thought you said they didn't come this close to Wishing Moon Bay."

"They don't." He let out a long breath. "But it wasn't Ivan. I'm sure it wasn't. It didn't feel like him."

"But it felt like a dragon?" She reached for his hand, needing to feel connected to him, needing to feel safe. Yet she doubted that Rift would keep her safe if a dragon attacked them. A snow leopard wasn't any match for a dragon. No other creature was.

Unless they were small. Perhaps Ivan shifted into a small dragon no bigger than a bird.

"It felt like a dragon." He tilted his head back and stared at the sky, but his eyes were unfocused. "Whatever it was, it's gone."

"We should get back." The spell between them was broken. Belle needed to get back and check on the children. "Are you going to tell your brother?"

Rift sighed and looked down at her face. "I don't know. He's wound up so tight after this afternoon. Learning that he has treasure and that someone else is trying to get it has hit him hard. He's got so many questions and so far, no answers."

"I know how he feels." Belle cupped his face in her hands and kissed his lips. "Come on. We both have our families to check in on."

"You're right." Rift threaded his fingers through her hair and didn't move as he searched her face. "There's something I want to say first."

"Oh, this sounds ominous." She tried to laugh but it died on her lips. His eyes darkened as he stared at her.

"I know it's a little premature, but I wanted to tell you that I love you, Belle. I was worried if I said it before, I might frighten you away. But you get it now. I know you understand the shifter bond and I believe you feel it, too." He was deadly serious.

"I do get it." She placed her hand on her heart. "And I think I feel it, too, although part of me believes it's just wishful thinking."

"It might be my wishful thinking." He grinned and the mood shifted, the intensity in his eyes fading.

"It's too soon for me to say I love you." She pressed her lips together as if to keep herself from saying those words. They were there on her lips. All she had to do was open her mouth and they would spill out. So why did she stop them?

"I didn't say it to pressure you into saying it back," he told her. "I just wanted you to know. I needed to say it. I needed to tell you I love you." He shrugged. "So you have something to hold onto. To believe in if things get crazy."

She placed her hand on his chest and stroked him through his shirt. "One thing we both know is that things are going to get crazy in the next few days."

"I can't think of anyone I'd rather face that with." He took her hand and they walked back up the beach toward the car. "But if I could spare you any of this, I would."

"I know. But what doesn't kill us makes us stronger and this is not going to kill us. I'm done with the ghosts of my father and my uncle hanging over me. And my mom. I hate seeing the guilt in her eyes. It's like she blames herself for all of this."

"It's not her fault."

"And Ivan? Do you think he'll ever rest if we don't find out the truth about his treasure?"

"I don't know much about dragons, but Ivan is one of the most levelheaded people I've ever met. He'll get over it, I'm sure." They reached the car and he paused, holding both her hands in his. "If Ivan didn't sense the dragon, I'm not going to tell him. Not yet."

"I think that's a sound idea. One problem at a time." She kissed his cheek. "Thanks for a wonderful evening."

"Did it clear your head?" Rift got into the passenger seat and closed the door as she put the key in the ignition.

"Oh, now my head is filled with thoughts of a perfect kiss." She smiled shyly. "Because that's what it was, Rift. Perfect."

As she drove away from the beach, he smiled to himself, his eyes glinting in the moonlight.

A grin spread across her face. She might not be able to admit it to him yet, but she did love him.

Even though it seemed impossible to fall for a stranger, she had. Totally and completely.

20

RIFT

"Thanks for coming, Oscar." Rift met the retired police detective outside the hotel. He had been the reason Rift had found his mate even though it hadn't been intentional. Now he was here to help find a way to keep Belle and her family safe.

"You're welcome, Rift. Anything to help." He patted Rift on the back. "I can't tell you how happy I was to hear that you found your mate. That toy has been sitting in police evidence all these years. If we hadn't decided to use it to help track down Murray, you might never have met Belle."

"You don't have to remind me." Rift looked up at the hotel. He could sense Belle in her room. She was alone with Katrina since the children had gone to play with Milo. Penny had taken them along with a picnic down to the beach. "I'm going to have nightmares about it, I'm sure."

"You mean if you hadn't decided to go with Aiden and Caleb?" Oscar followed Rift into the hotel.

"Yes. Just a small change of plans and I'd have never met her." He shuddered. "It's a scary thought."

"And one you shouldn't dwell on. Fate meant for you to

meet. And fate means for you to stay together. There's a reason you met, and my guess is you are supposed to help her figure this whole mess out." Oscar patted the briefcase in his hand. "I wish I had more answers for you."

"We didn't expect you to solve this. Anything you can tell us will help. Katrina, Belle's mom, has no idea what this is all about. But part of me wonders if it's buried in her head somewhere. If her brother or Belle's father gave her a clue." Maybe Rift was hoping for a miracle so that they could resolve the issue and then move on with their lives.

Now that they knew Belle would happily move to Wishing Moon Bay, it was hard to be patient. Both he and his snow leopard wanted to experience living with Belle and the children. He wanted them to settle here and become part of the ever-growing family Valerie had made when she adopted six boys so long ago.

"Have you thought about asking Silas for his help?" Oscar's suggestion of asking a vampire for help didn't sit easily with Rift. It wasn't that he didn't trust in the vampire's abilities to dig out the information, it was more of a concern as to the cost.

Silas has already extracted promises from Logan, Penny, Dario, and Helena. Rift didn't want the whole of the family to owe Silas a favor. One he could call on at any time.

"I'll think about it. Although, I don't want to pile too much on them at once. Belle had no idea shifters existed until yesterday. Or fae."

"And vampires don't exactly have a great reputation in the world beyond. All those movies about cold blood-sucking creatures. They should learn some facts," Oscar said.

"Vampires are cold bloodsuckers," Rift reminded him. "They're just not so prone to killing callously for their next meal."

"Maybe we'll use Silas as a last resort." Oscar chuckled.

"Do you ever wonder what would happen if everyone in the world beyond found out that all those supernatural beings they're afraid of are real?"

"We all think that from time to time. Shifters would be judged like the werewolves in movies. All fur and fangs." He made his hands into claws as if he were about to pounce on Oscar. His actions were met with a raised eyebrow from Jeremy as they entered the reception area. Rift instantly let his hands drop to his sides when he saw the two guests watching him.

His snow leopard laughed at Rift's embarrassment. *How old are you?*

Young enough to still know how to have fun, Rift retorted. Maybe he'd been hanging around with kids too long. He loved to play chase with Milo, who loved the shifter to act fierce and scary before he wrestled him to the ground.

"Where are we meeting?" Oscar asked as they crossed the reception area.

Rift was distracted for a moment, his attention drawn to the next floor. Belle and her mom were on their way downstairs. He could sense her getting closer and closer.

"I know that look." Oscar nudged his friend. "I can't wait to meet your mate."

"I can't wait for you to meet her." Rift headed for the stairs as if he were drawn to Belle by some invisible force.

He held his breath as he waited for her to appear. They'd only spoken briefly this morning when he went to get Jack and Rosie. He'd dropped them off at the beach where they'd joined Penny and Milo for their picnic.

While he was out, the two women had gone through Reggie's things one more time. If they had found something new, Belle hadn't shared the news with him.

Why are you so nervous? His snow leopard was in tune with Rift's moods.

I'm just worried that things might have changed since last night. That I might have gone too fast when I told her that I loved her. He winced inwardly. She might not have been ready to hear it. Not from a man she'd only just met.

On the contrary, his snow leopard replied, I think it's exactly what she needed to hear. She knows we're meant to be together. Now she understands how strong our feelings are toward her. She won't be second-guessing.

As Belle came into view, her eyes sought him out and a smile instantly spread over her beautiful face. Rift smiled back. He imagined he looked like an idiot grinning from ear to ear, but he didn't care. Belle made his heart sing, and he wanted the world to know she was his.

And we are hers, his snow leopard reminded him.

Rift glanced sideways at Oscar. For an instant, all thoughts of his mate disappeared. "Oscar?"

"Hmm." Oscar dragged his eyes away from the two women who were halfway down the stairs.

"Is there something you need to tell me?" Rift cocked an eyebrow at Oscar.

"No." Oscar shook his head. "Why don't you introduce us and then we should go get started? We have a lot to cover."

"Okay." Rift still wasn't sure Oscar was being truthful when he said he had nothing to tell. The guy had been staring at Katrina in the same way Rift had stared at Belle when they first met. "Belle, Katrina. This is Oscar. Oscar..."

"Belle and Katrina." The older man's eyes crinkled at the corners as he smiled and held out his hand. "Good to meet you both."

"Good to meet you, Oscar." Katrina smiled shyly. "I believe it's you we have to thank for Rift finding my daughter."

"Oh, the toy. It was the only link we had to the man who kidnapped Aiden and Caleb. I'd never have guessed it would have ended up in such a happy outcome. But it seems right somehow. That bad things that happened in the past can lead to good things in the future." Oscar's eyes seemed to fix on Katrina, who blushed as if not used to being the center of anyone's attention.

"I suppose that counts for Ivan, too," Belle said. "He's learned something about his parents and his treasure. Although I'm not sure he sees it as a good thing."

"We should go. Ivan is waiting with Valerie in her apartment. I'm sure he'll want to hear if you have any news." Rift lingered for a moment, he wanted to hold Belle's hand, to kiss her lips and whisper I love you in her ear. But her mom stuck to her side and so he turned away and led them down the hallway to Valerie's private apartment.

As soon as they reached the door, he sensed Ivan coming toward them. The door swung open before Rift had a chance to turn the handle. Ivan stood before them looking disheveled, as if he hadn't slept and there was a haunted expression in his eyes that Rift had never seen before.

He's not in great shape, Rift's snow leopard commented. Do you think he sensed the dragon flying close to shore last night, too?

I have no idea. Rift had spoken to Ivan briefly last night after he and Belle returned to the hotel. Ivan hadn't mentioned the other dragon and Rift hadn't found a subtle way to broach the subject.

"There you are." Ivan's eyes glowed amber as he greeted them, but he instantly took a deep breath and calmed himself. His eyes returned to their normal color, even though they were still wild, a little unfocused, and red-rimmed.

"Here we are." Rift positioned himself between Ivan and the others. Was his brother a danger to them?

"Mom has some fresh coffee on, and I baked some pastries." Ivan regained control of his emotions and stepped back to allow them to enter.

"The pastries smell wonderful," Katrina said politely but avoided eye contact with Ivan.

"Ivan. How are you?" Oscar was never one to hide away from the truth.

"I've been better," Ivan admitted. "I left the tiara at home to see if a little distance helped but it's like I can hear it calling me."

"I don't know much about dragon treasure," Oscar said. "But from what I've read, it'll get easier. Usually, you're raised knowing the treasure. A young dragon shifter handles it, gets used to the feel of it both physically and mentally before his first shift. Unfortunately, you've never felt your treasure and so it's a shock. Like a drug that you can't resist."

"That explains a lot." Ivan went into the kitchen where Valerie was pouring coffee. "I wanted to apologize for my behavior yesterday." Ivan directed his words to Belle. "I never meant to upset your children. Or scare them."

"I get that. Apology accepted. Even though I don't think Rosie noticed your behavior, she was just upset that she couldn't keep the tiara. But I warned her it probably belonged to someone else, and she couldn't keep it." Belle took a plate and one of the offered pastries. "These look so good."

"They melt in your mouth." Oscar took a bite and rolled his eyes in pleasure. Whatever his first impression of Katrina had been, he also seemed to have gotten his emotions under control.

It sure is like the world has gone crazy, his snow leopard said.

And it's going to get crazier. Rift ate a pastry, certain he was going to need the sugar rush to get him through this morning. Ivan barely looked as if he was hanging onto his sanity, let alone his emotions. Every time his treasure was mentioned, his eyes flashed amber and there was a hunger there for more than a sweet pastry.

"What new information do you have?" Valerie asked when everyone had eaten, and their coffee cups refilled.

"Right." Oscar placed his briefcase down on the countertop and opened it up. "I spent hours searching for any information on Murray and Reggie that might be a clue to where the tiara came from. I also tried to cross-reference it to the details surrounding both Ivan's adoption and that of the twins."

"And did you find anything?" Belle asked.

"Not much." Oscar took a piece of paper out of the briefcase and set it down on the countertop. "This drawing was made from a witness statement. It is the prime suspect in Murray's murder. Although he was never found."

"He looks familiar." Katrina picked up the image and took a closer look. Placing her hand over the mouth, she squinted. "He shares a resemblance to one of the men who came to the house." She handed it to Belle. "Do you recognize him from the truck?"

"He's the guy who grabbed me." She took the photo and turned it around so Rift could see it. "Do you recognize him?"

Rift's jaw tensed and his hands curled into fists. "Yes, it's not the same guy, but the resemblance is uncanny. Perhaps he was this guy's son?"

"That would make sense. It seems your family and his family have history." Oscar glanced at Ivan. "And your family."

"And the twins," Valerie added. "It's like a spiderweb, so many threads all woven together."

"It's time we picked them apart." Katrina tilted her chin up. "And ended this."

"Where do we start?" Ivan asked.

"That's the question we need to answer," Oscar replied.

"Rift said you boxed up all the stuff from your brother's house. May I go through it?"

"We've been through it all several times. We can't find anything that might help us," Katrina replied. "But you're more than welcome to take a look."

Oscar nodded. "If I may. The photo helps us identify the people involved, but something is missing. We have no idea what these people have to do with the tiara. Or how a piece of Ivan's family treasure ended up in the middle of all of this."

"That's what I'd like to know the answer to," Ivan said. "How did the tiara end up in Reggie's possession? Was he responsible for my parents' death and Aiden and Caleb's parents?"

"It's looking that way," Oscar agreed reluctantly. He glanced at Katrina and then Belle, but there was nothing but kindness and sympathy in his expression.

"Whatever you need, just ask. We'll do whatever it takes to get to the bottom of this. No matter what." Katrina took a shaky breath.

"It's okay, Mom." Belle put her arm around her mom's shoulders.

"It's not, though, is it?" Katrina swallowed hard. "If I hadn't run away from your father, I might have been able to prevent some of the awful things Reggie and Murray did. I would have seen things..."

"You don't know that. Dad and Uncle Reggie were good at hiding things and covering up what they were involved in." Belle kissed her mom on the cheek. "Come on, have some more coffee, and then we'll go through Reggie's things one more time."

"Belle's right, Katrina," Oscar said softly. "I was a detective for a long time. I've met families in similar circumstances who had no idea about what was going on."

"I just hope we might find what you need in Reginald's

belongings." Katrina accepted a coffee refill from Valerie. "Thanks."

"And if we don't?" Ivan asked.

Oscar straightened his back. "Then we'll find another way. But rest assured, we will solve this mystery." He glanced at Katrina. "One way or another, this has to end."

21

BELLE

"Do you see anything that might help us?" Belle hovered over Oscar as he leafed through the books from Reggie's house one more time.

"No." Oscar didn't hide his disappointment. "I really thought there would be something here."

"Okay, I think we've wasted enough time on this." Belle straightened up. "Why don't you tell us what you know, and we'll try to figure out a plan. We can't stay here forever."

She glanced up at Rift. She hadn't meant it the way it sounded, and she flashed him a brief smile, wanting to assure him her mind hadn't changed. Their life was here in Wishing Moon Bay, but only after this was over.

Some things needed arranging, like transferring schools and working her notice at her job. Belle wasn't going to just disappear into the night with no explanation. People would worry about her, there would be a police investigation which would cost time and money that was best spent solving real crimes.

Not that this wasn't a real crime, her family was being threatened. That was their reality.

And all because of her father and uncle.

"Okay, let's move on." Oscar restacked the books, giving the boxes containing Reggie's stuff one last reproachful look before he stood up. "Let's keep it all for now, though."

"You think there's something we've all missed?" Katrina asked.

Oscar turned to face her, his eyes soft as he smiled lightly. "Who knows. But the toy that led us to you had been sitting in an evidence locker for decades. No one had a clue as to how important it was."

"Point taken," Katrina conceded.

"Let's go see what else you've got, Oscar." Rift patted the detective on the shoulder.

"It's not going to be helpful in tracking down the guys who threatened you all." Oscar shook his head. "As I said, the guy in the photo has never been found. The chances of us tracking these guys down in a short space of time is slim at best."

"What if we bait a trap?" Katrina's suggestion was met with silence from the others.

"I doubt they'd fall for that. Not after we ambushed them in the forest," Rift replied.

"They want what they think we have," Katrina replied.

"Maybe they believed us?" Belle folded her arms across her body. "Maybe they believed me when I told them we don't have their treasure."

Rift huffed and covered his mouth with his hand. "We could be doing all this for nothing."

"We could." Katrina glanced at Belle. "We need to go home."

Oscar shook his head. "It's too risky. Unless you have a contingency plan, it's too risky."

"We're never going to find out if we don't try," Belle told him.

"Let's go to Valerie's apartment and discuss this calmly." Rift moved to Belle's side and slipped his arm around her shoulders, pulling her close. "Whatever you decide, the children should stay here."

Belle leaned into him and nodded. "I agree. They'll be safe here. Do you think Penny would look after them for a couple of days?" She hated the idea of leaving her children with a stranger, but she trusted Rift and Rift trusted Penny.

"I'm sure between Penny and Helena, they can cope." He pressed his lips together. "I don't like the idea of you being in danger."

She turned to face him and placed her hand on his chest. "But you do like the idea of me living here in Wishing Moon Bay."

He cracked a smile. "I do. And you won't be happy here if you are always looking over your shoulder, worrying that they might find a way in."

"Exactly. I want the kids to be safe and have their freedom. If we don't resolve this or at least convince ourselves that they've given up on us, then I'm going to be watching the kids like a hawk in case someone tries to snatch them." She shuddered and he placed his hand on the nape of her neck, pulling her toward him before he dropped a kiss on the top of her head.

"Let's talk and then I'll make arrangements with Penny." They followed the others back to Valerie's apartment.

"Did you find anything?" Valerie asked hopefully as they entered.

"No." Oscar sighed as he went to his briefcase which was still on the counter where he'd left it. "At least if there's a clue in there, I can't fit it together with the rest of the puzzle."

Valerie handed him a cup of coffee. "If anyone can figure this out, it's you, Oscar. There might not be a clue in there at all."

"I know, I was hoping. Because the other information we have is not enough to track these guys down." He flipped open his briefcase and took out a folder. "You've seen the photo. We now know there is a link between the person who is wanted for Murray's murder and the person who attacked Belle."

"We do," Rift agreed.

"I've also managed to get hold of Reginald's bank statements." Oscar side-eyed Katrina. "Not through official channels, I hope that's not going to be an issue."

"No, it's not," Katrina confirmed. "Do they tell us anything helpful?"

"They show that Reginald made a regular payment that seems to be for a storage box at a bank close to the address where he lived before he was sent to prison."

"He paid for a storage box for all of those years?" Rift asked.

"He did. I don't think it's unusual. If he had anything of value, it would have been stored there safely ready for when he got out of prison." Oscar glanced at Katrina once more. "Did he leave anything with you?"

"No." She shook her head and lowered her gaze. "I know I was his sister, but we weren't speaking at the time. I was trying to build a life for me and my daughter."

Oscar smiled gently. "You did a good job from what I can see."

"I tried but it's not been easy leaving the past behind. Even now, my name is linked to Reggie's." She cupped her hands around her coffee cup and drank, her eyes fixed on the floor.

"Do the bank statements tell us anything else?" Belle asked.

"No. Only that he rented a house when he left prison and at that time, he stopped the payment to the bank."

"So Reggie went to the bank and took out whatever he'd been storing there." There were no prizes for guessing what that was. What had he planned to do with it? Sell it? Belle frowned as she mulled this information over. Reggie's health had deteriorated so rapidly. "Do you have anything else?"

"No." Oscar seemed a little embarrassed. "I need more time to make inquiries."

"Thanks, Oscar." Belle pushed herself away from the counter. "We appreciate what you've told us."

"It's not a lot." Oscar put the folder back in his briefcase. "And I have reached out to some old contacts. So there's a chance I might get some more news. Particularly news of the photo. I've asked a colleague to run it through photo recognition software. Technology has evolved so much since Murray was murdered."

"That sounds hopeful," Belle conceded.

"In the meantime, we need to go back home and try to flush out the people who ambushed us." Katrina drained her coffee cup and went to the sink. "Thanks for your hospitality, Valerie."

"I'd ask if you were sure you were doing the right thing," Valerie replied. "but I can see from your expressions that you've made up your minds."

"We have," Belle confirmed.

"I'm done running." Katrina puffed out her chest and straightened her back. "I ran once before to make a fresh start. I'm not doing it again. Not when we have no idea what we're up against. Belle is right. I don't want us to spend the rest of our lives looking over our shoulders."

"That's not going to happen," Rift told her. "With Oscar's skills and his connections, and a bunch of shifters alongside you, these guys can't hide forever."

"What I'd like to know," Valerie began, "is how they found out about the treasure."

Rift switched his attention to his mom. “Do you have an idea about that?”

“No, not really. I had no idea about the treasure.” Valerie shrugged. “Of course, it makes sense that his family did have treasure, most dragon shifters do. But there was no trace as far as I am aware.”

“And dragons don’t exactly go around showing off their treasure, do they?” Oscar replied. “So how did a group of people in the world beyond Wishing Moon Bay know about it?”

“And how did my father and uncle know about it?” Belle mused.

“Perhaps that’s what we should focus on.” Oscar flipped open his briefcase once more and took out the photo. He placed it down on the counter and stared at it, his eyes a little out of focus. “Who are you? And why did you kill Murray?”

Rift cleared his throat and Oscar jerked his head back, his eyes going from Belle to Katrina.

“It’s okay. You can talk openly in front of us both. I think we’re both somewhat emotionally unattached to Murray,” Katrina assured them.

“I never knew him.” Belle’s jaw clenched. “Honestly, when people talk about him, they might as well be talking about a stranger.” She put her hand over her heart. “Rightly or wrongly, I have no love for him.”

“Okay.” Oscar nodded again. “I want to focus on trying to figure out why Murray was murdered. I’ll go over the case notes one more time. It was thought that it was a revenge killing. So revenge for what?”

“It would take a lifetime to figure that one out,” Katrina said drily. “This is a man who kidnapped children, for goodness’ sake. Who knows what other heinous crimes he’s committed?”

"True." Oscar rubbed his chin. "But this must be connected to the death of Ivan's parents."

"I believe you're right," Valerie agreed.

"If we can make the connection, we'll be able to figure it all out." Oscar closed his briefcase and lifted it off the counter. "Thank you for the coffee, Valerie. I'll go and nudge things along. I'll call all my contacts and sift through the information. As soon as I know something, I'll let you know."

"Thank you, Oscar." Tears pricked Belle's eyes as she went to the detective and hugged him. "You've been so incredibly kind and helpful."

"It's what I do." He looked embarrassed as he put his arms around her, his touch light on her shoulders. "It's what I've always done. I thought when I retired, I might have taken things easy, but it's in my blood. I want to make things right for as many people as possible."

"If there's ever anything you need, Oscar, ask. We owe you a big debt." Katrina held herself back and didn't hug the detective when Belle let him go.

There was something in her mom's eyes, a glimmer of hope, of wanting, perhaps even longing as she looked at Oscar and then quickly turned her attention to her empty coffee cup.

"Thanks, Oscar." Rift shook his hand. "We all owe you."

"I don't do this so that you owe me," Oscar replied. "I do it because it's right. I've watched you all grow up. I'm proud of the men you've become. To see you all happy with your mates is thanks enough."

"Except Ivan," Valerie murmured, and Rift smiled sadly at his mom. The dragon shifter seemed to have gotten the raw deal in all of this.

Or perhaps, in his eyes, finding a piece of his treasure was more than compensation for a mate. Belle dismissed the thought immediately. To a shifter, their mate was everything.

They meant more than life itself. She shivered. There was no way another life was being lost because of her family and the secrets of the past.

22

RIFT

"When do we leave?" Rift gathered all the cups and put them in the sink before he turned around. Oscar had left Valerie's apartment and it was time to make firm plans.

"We need to pack. If you could talk to Penny, that would be great. If she says yes, then I need to explain everything to the children." Belle's throat constricted and she covered her eyes with her hand. "Sorry." She sniffed loudly and straightened up.

"There's nothing to be sorry for," Valerie said kindly. "Your kids are the most important thing in the world. You want to protect them."

"I do." She wiped her fingers under her eyes. "Which is why we need to leave."

"Why don't you both go talk to Penny?" Katrina suggested. "I can pack our stuff." She gave a small laugh. "There's not exactly a lot of it. We only planned to be out for the day."

"Good idea." Rift nodded toward the door. "We can go to

the beach and join them. I'll ask Penny while you spend some time with the kids."

Belle's mouth turned down at the corners, but she nodded. "I'd like that. If you don't mind, Mom."

"No, go look at the ocean. See your children playing happily. It'll make it easier, I can tell you." Katrina hugged her daughter. "Go on."

Belle hesitated for a moment and then followed Rift out of the apartment. He paused as he closed the door behind them and offered her his hand. He wanted to tell her it would all be okay, but they were empty words, none of them knew what they would face once they put their plan in motion.

Maybe she's right and those guys believed her when she said they didn't have the tiara. She was telling the truth, after all, his snow leopard said.

I'd like to believe that's true but until we have proof...

If Belle moves her family here, all we have to do is keep her safe in the world beyond for a few weeks. Then they'll be safe forever. His snow leopard's chest rumbled at the thought of their new family coming to live in Wishing Moon Bay.

"If Penny agrees to look after the children while we're away, I'll arrange for them to come by the hotel and pick up their stuff," Rift said, more to make conversation than anything. Belle looked tense, her mouth turned down at the corners as she nodded in agreement.

"At least I can go home and grab some clothes and things to bring back. When we come back..." Her voice trailed off.

"Hey, we'll be back before we know it." He wrapped his arm around her shoulder and pulled her close as they headed out of the hotel through one of the rear doors used by the staff.

She snorted. "And it's not as if my kids will miss me. They'll be having too much fun."

"You know how much they love you," Rift replied. "I see it

in their eyes every time they look at you. You are the center of their world."

"Thanks, Rift. I needed to hear that." She wiped her hand across her cheeks. "It's tough being on my own. I wonder how my mom did it. I mean, my kids had their father in their lives until a few months ago. And if things got really bad, I hope he'd be there for them. But she was completely on her own."

"And you have her strength and determination." They crossed the parking lot, and she dug her car keys out of her purse. "You've passed that same strength and determination on to your children. Watching them work together to build the sandcastle the other day, they worked together and helped each other."

"The bond between them and between the three of us has grown stronger since their dad left. I worry it's because they're afraid I might leave, too." She tried to smile but the corners of her mouth were still downturned.

"They know you are there for them. If they were worried you were going to leave, they'd be telling you that you're the greatest storyteller, or they would cling to you as if they're afraid you might disappear." He rested his hand on the roof of the car. "That's how I felt when I first came here to Valerie. I was afraid to let her out of my sight. Afraid to lose her love."

Belle closed the space between them and nestled against him, her body pressed against his as she wound her arms around his waist. "She's an amazing woman. I hope I can be half the mother she is. And, if you're sure she needs help and you aren't just inventing a job for me, I'd be honored to work with her. I can learn a lot from her."

Rift brushed her hair back from her face and lowered his head, capturing her lips in a searing kiss. Heat flared across his skin as she cupped his cheek in her hand. Things were falling into place. It was as if he were standing on the threshold of the rest of his life and all he needed to do was step forward and he'd have it all, all his dreams come true.

Yet there was an invisible hand holding onto him, keeping him from taking that step.

"We should go," he murmured against her cheek.

"We should." She ran her tongue along her lower lip and sighed heavily before she pulled away from him and went around to the driver's side of the car and got inside.

Rift took a moment to steady himself. Belle affected his senses like nothing else he'd ever experienced. It was like she swept him off his feet and raised him into the air where he hovered six feet off the ground.

Just get in the car, his snow leopard said.

Rift snapped his head back and opened the car door. Sliding into the passenger seat, his senses were once more overwhelmed by her nearness. But he had to regain control. Their safety, once they left Wishing Moon Bay, might depend on it.

Ten minutes later, Belle and Rift were walking hand in hand along the beach searching for Penny and the children.

"There they are." Rift pointed toward a cave entrance. He'd texted Penny and she'd told him they were picnicking inside one of the caves. The children were pretending to be pirates searching for buried treasure.

Dragon treasure, his snow leopard said. I wonder if this is where the rest of Ivan's treasure is buried.

If it was this close, I'm sure he could sense it, Rift answered. Logan said Ivan has been testing how far his senses stretch when it comes to locating his treasure. It's farther than our senses usually stretch. The treasure is like a part of him, he shares a connection with it that's almost like the one between mates.

When this is over and Belle is safe, maybe we should help him track down the rest of it. Perhaps the guys after Belle might be able to give us more details. His snow leopard extended his claws. I could help loosen their tongues.

If that's what Ivan wants, we'll do what we can, Rift confirmed. He needed to talk with Ivan as soon as possible. He'd been so wrapped up in his problems that he hadn't been there for his brother.

Ivan understands, his snow leopard said.

"Hey, how are you guys doing?" Belle waved and ran toward the children as they played on the rocks surrounding the cave entrance.

"Mommy!" Rosie had a towel tied around her neck like a cape and as she jumped off the rocks and landed on the soft sand, her eyes shone bright with happiness.

This is how childhood should be, Rift's snow leopard said. Filled with happiness and adventures on the beach, just like our childhood.

There was so much they both wanted to share with the children. So many sights to see and memories to make.

"Hey there. You look as if you're having fun!" Belle caught her daughter in her arms and swung her around.

"We're looking for treasure!" Jack brandished a long stick like a sword.

"Did you find any?" Belle went to the children, while Rift headed into the mouth of the cave where Penny was seated on a blanket, a book lying next to her.

"Hi, you." Penny patted the blanket next to her. "Are you hungry?"

"Always." Rift helped himself to the chicken salad sandwiches Penny offered him.

"Whatever it is, the answer is yes." She eyed him curiously as he bit into the sandwich.

He chewed quickly and then swallowed. "Am I that transparent?"

"I figured you want me to look after the kids while you

leave town." Her jaw clenched as she watched him. "You need to figure this all out so your mate will be safe and that's not going to happen here, is it?"

"No, it's not." He took another bite of his sandwich while watching Belle as she picked up a stick and pretended to fight with Jack. "Are you sure you don't mind?"

"We'll manage between us. You know we'll all pitch in. Helena will love to have the three of them over to her house. Call it a trial run for when she has her own brood of children. Although, it might be a baptism by fire." She chuckled. "But they're good kids."

"This whole thing seems to be a baptism by fire." He finished his sandwich and drew his knees up to his chest. "You'd think one of us might get it easy when we meet our mate."

"Perhaps it'll be Ivan." She glanced sideways at him. "How is he doing?"

"He's been better. It's like there's this other side of him that none of us knew about." Rift wrapped his arms around his knees as Belle dropped to the ground, feigning a mortal wound.

"It's like when you find your mate. Things shift in your head. It's like being thrown into the ocean and forced to learn how to swim. The waves wash over you and you have to fight to take a breath." She sucked in the salty sea air. "At least that's how it felt to me."

"You're right." He stared out to sea for a long moment. "I'm scared that now that Ivan has a taste of his treasure, he might not be able to come back to us, come back to how he used to be unless he finds the rest of it."

"Logan is worried, too. I suspect we'll all need to be there for Ivan. We'll all need to support him through this in the same way he's supported us through everything." She touched Rift's arm. "He'll always be your brother, that will never change."

Rift turned to face Penny. "I'll do whatever it takes to help him find his treasure. But I don't want it to consume him. I don't want this hunger to take control of him."

"It won't. Not while he has his family by his side, and we are always going to be by his side." Penny laughed as Jack and Milo ran along the beach yelling in victory while Rosie knelt down and kissed her mom's cheek. "I am in love with that little girl."

"Me, too," Rift admitted.

"You'll make a wonderful father, Rift. Milo loves you so much. You're the fun uncle. He loves playing with you. They're incredibly lucky." Penny patted his back.

He turned to look at her and rested his head on his knee. "I'm the lucky one. This is more than I could ever have wished for."

"Then maybe you need to make bigger wishes. You deserve it."

Rift watched as Belle and Rosie came toward them. At that moment, he was the happiest man alive.

He wished that moment would last forever. But that wish was too big for anyone. Happiness couldn't last forever. No matter how many wish stones he threw in the ocean.

23

BELLE

"I can't thank Penny enough for agreeing to look after Rosie and Jack." Belle took one last look at the children as they climbed into Penny's car and waved goodbye.

"One day we can return the favor." Rift grinned as he waved before getting into Belle's car. It touched her heart that Rosie and Jack already responded to him. "Not that they'd expect it. They know how tough it is when you have kids. I watched Milo a lot when they were getting the candy store ready for opening."

"You do like children, don't you?" Belle drove away from the beach, they were heading back to the hotel where they would pick up Katrina. The plan was for them to go home and hopefully lure the bad guys out.

What happened then was still undecided. Rift couldn't take them all on alone, and Belle hated to ask his brothers to get involved.

"I do. Maybe because I'm still one myself." He grinned, he sure did have a boyish charm. One that made her heart melt and her stomach flip. If this wasn't love, she didn't know what it was.

"It's good that you're still in touch with that part of yourself. Having kids makes me look at things differently. It's like learning about life and the world around us all over again." She drove the car into the hotel parking lot and switched off the engine.

"Ivan." His expression sobered as the dragon shifter strode out of the hotel to meet them.

"Does he usually look that intense?" Belle asked.

"I'm not sure what Ivan's *usual* is anymore." Rift got out of the car and kept his body language neutral, even though his desire to protect his mate was overwhelming. And by Ivan's expression, protecting his mate against his brother might be exactly what Rift needed to do.

"I've been waiting for you to get back." Ivan stopped a few feet away from the car as if sensing Rift's unease.

"We went to the beach to check on the children and ask Penny if she could watch them while we're away. Did Valerie update you on the situation?" Rift went around the car and stood by Belle's side.

"She did. Which is why I was waiting for you." He took a couple of steps closer, his expression pained as he held out his hand. "I want you to take this."

The tiara sparkled as the sunlight hit it. Ivan must have spent hours cleaning it and restoring the luster to the gems. Belle's fingers grazed Rift's as she leaned closer to him, her heart hammering in her chest. As she glanced sideways at Rift, his confusion matched hers.

"Take it?" Rift didn't move, unsure of what Ivan meant.

"Yes. This is what those guys are looking for. I want you to take it and give it to them." His fingers clenched the tiara for a second before he reached for Rift's free hand. Inhumanly fast, Ivan shoved the tiara into his brother's hand and then took a few steps back.

"Ivan, this is yours. It might be the only family treasure you ever have. It's too important to you," Rift took a step forward, his hand outstretched.

Ivan put his hand up. "No!" He licked his lips. "I'm sorry I overreacted when I first sensed the treasure." He swallowed hard, his eyes lingering on the tiara before he raised his eyes to look at Belle. "Now I understand that it's just an object. It's not a person. It's not a mate. Or family. If this is what it takes to make sure you and your family safe, then I give it to you."

"Ivan, I don't know what to say." Belle covered her mouth with her hand.

"You don't have to say anything," he assured her. "I'd give all of my treasure if it meant keeping my family safe. And you are part of my family now."

"Ivan." Rift passed the tiara to Belle and then opened his arms to hug his brother. "I can't tell you how much this means to me."

"I know how much you all mean to me, so I have some idea." He clamped his arms around Rift and held him tightly. "I don't want you to go alone."

"We'll be okay," Rift assured him.

"I want to come with you. I've asked Elise and she's agreed to run the hotel restaurant for a few days. She's done it before while I visited Fiona and her family." He licked his lips again as he pulled away. "I'd also like to check out the house Reggie rented to see if there's any more treasure hidden there."

"That's a great idea," Rift agreed. "You would be able to sense it."

"It sure beats us trying to dig up the whole backyard," Belle added.

"Whatever I can do to help, I'll do it," Ivan said. "Afterward, I might go stay with Fiona for a while. I need to get some idea of what treasure means to a dragon and how to control these turbulent emotions. But first, I want to help you."

Rift nodded. "I'd like you to join us." He glanced at Belle, who nodded. "I was worried I might not be able to keep Belle and Katrina safe on my own and I don't want to ask the others." He glanced toward the hotel. "I know they'd come in a heartbeat, but I don't want them to risk their lives or their mates."

Ivan held out his arms and forced a grin on his face. "That's why you can take me. I am mate-free."

"That doesn't make you dispensable," Rift reminded him.

"More dispensable than you." Ivan arched his eyebrow, the color had returned to his cheeks and he looked more like his old self even though his gaze kept dropping to the tiara in Belle's hand.

"Okay." Rift nodded. "We can take my car and Belle and Katrina can go in theirs."

"Oscar is coming, too." Ivan's news was met with curiosity. "He's arranging backup. He said it would be easier to keep us all up to date if we travel together." Ivan shrugged. "He's the expert on these things, I'm just going along with it."

"He does have contacts in the police force," Rift said. "I guess it would be easier for him to call in backup if we need it."

"He likes your mom." Ivan leaned to the side and looked past Rift. "I can see it in his eyes and hear it in his voice when he talks to her."

Rift chuckled. "I had picked up on that, too."

Belle's hand fluttered to her mouth and she hid a smile. "I thought it was just me." She shook her head and approached them cautiously. "Please, don't say anything or make fun."

Ivan frowned and shook his head. "We wouldn't. If there's

one thing you can bank on, it's that a shifter will do anything to ensure the course of true love runs smooth."

"I like shifters more and more." Belle grinned but kept the tiara out of sight of Ivan. She wasn't ready to completely trust the dragon shifter yet. Not when it came to his treasure.

"Come on. We should get going." Ivan patted Rift on the shoulder and pointed to the tiara. "Keep that in your car. If we get split up or if anything happens, just hand it over to those guys."

Belle nodded. "Thank you, Ivan. I know how hard this must be for you."

Ivan nodded. "I'm not saying that I won't hunt them down and get it back. But I'm working on my anger issues in that department. I was totally unprepared when I sensed the tiara. It was as if someone had taken a part of me."

"And if you don't get it back?" Belle asked.

Ivan shrugged. "I lived without it before, I can again."

Belle twisted the tiara around in her hand, but she kept it hidden behind her back. "I don't want you to condemn yourself to a life of misery over this. We will find another way."

Ivan shook his head. "No." He placed his hand on his chest. "That isn't who I want to be. I don't want to be held prisoner by a piece of gold and jewels."

Belle laughed softly. "You don't have to be a dragon shifter with treasure to be held prisoner by an expensive piece of jewelry."

"I've made up my mind," Ivan insisted. "But I appreciate your concern."

"Of course, you're family now." She leveled her gaze at him.

"We are," he agreed. "And this family needs to get on the road."

"We do." Belle nodded toward the hotel. "Do you know if my mom is ready?"

"She's been waiting for a while. She's talking to Valerie and Oscar." He stepped toward the hotel. "Come on, I've already loaded my pack into Oscar's car."

"He's driving?" Rift followed Ivan into the hotel and Belle followed. He preferred to keep between them just in case the need to grab his treasure overwhelmed Ivan.

Relax, he does have it under control, Rift's snow leopard assured him.

I don't want to take any chances, Rift replied, but he was certain Ivan was on his way back to his normal self. And, above all else, he was certain that Ivan would never do anything to hurt Belle or anyone else he cared about.

They headed around the back of the hotel and entered Valerie's apartment. Katrina and Oscar were seated in the living room, while Valerie was in the kitchen.

"Ah, there you are." Katrina jumped out of her seat as if she'd been caught misbehaving. "Did Penny agree to watch the children?"

"She did. And Ivan told us Oscar was coming, too." Belle met her mom's eyes, but Katrina looked away, suddenly finding whatever Valerie was doing in the kitchen intriguing.

"I am." Oscar's gaze followed Katrina as she darted out of the room. "I've been in contact with the police department near where you live. I have a contact there."

"You have contacts everywhere," Valerie called from the kitchen.

"I have been in this line of work for a long time." Oscar rolled his shoulders back. "I also managed to find someone who knew Aiden and Caleb's father. I briefly explained this had to do with his death and they are interested in helping, too." He arched an eyebrow. "Another shifter on the team might be useful."

"If he knew their dad, he must be old," Belle said.

"Shifters might get old, but they also get more cunning," Rift replied.

"I didn't mean to be rude." Belle's cheeks turned pink as she added, "I just don't want anyone to get hurt. Those guys might not have been shifters, but they knew how to handle themselves."

"They did. But last time we didn't shift. If things turn ugly, we have that option this time." Rift glanced at Ivan. "Or maybe not."

"Yeah, a dragon on the streets might be hard to explain." He shrugged. "But I can improvise."

Valerie came into the living room with Katrina. "I also talked to Karros and Zara. They are ready to help if you need them."

"Karros is Elise's brother and Zara is Caleb and Aiden's sister," Rift explained. "Long story, but they are mates."

"I don't want to get them hurt," Belle insisted.

"Zara is as much a victim of all this as her brothers. She wants to help you," Valerie insisted.

"Even though my father was responsible for what happened to her brothers?" Belle asked then she held up her hand. "Family. I get it."

"You are our family, yes. You had nothing to do with what your father did." Valerie handed a backpack to Rift. "Here, food for the trip. I've given a smaller pack to Katrina."

Ivan leaned forward and sniffed the pack. "Hmm, something smells good."

"That's a great compliment coming from my son, the chef." Valerie's eyes brimmed with tears as she held out her arms to him. "Take care of yourself. And don't do anything rash or stupid."

"Would I?" Ivan asked.

"I've been your mother for long enough to know the

answer to that." She arched her eyebrow as she let him go. "Look after each other."

"You sound like you did when we boys were going out on an adventure on the mountain or along the coast." Rift hugged Valerie and dropped a kiss on her cheek. "And I'll never get too old to hear it."

"I love you all." Valerie buried her face in his shoulder. "I just want you to come back safe. We all have so much to look forward to. We have a new generation to care for, Milo, Jack, and Rosie, and the new babies on the way. I don't want anything to cast a shadow over that."

"I'll make sure they all come back safe," Oscar promised, as if he would handle a fight better than a dragon shifter. And Belle liked the detective just a little bit more because of it.

"Okay, enough goodbyes. You need to go." Valerie let go of Rift and looked away for a moment as she wiped her fingers under her eyes. "I'm too old to get so emotional."

"I find the older I get, the more emotional I get," Katrina confessed as she too looked misty-eyed.

"Okay, Mom, you are with me. The guys are all in Oscar's car. We'll see you in a couple of hours." Belle linked her arms with her mom and guided her out of the apartment. "We'll see you soon, Valerie."

"I'll be waiting. And don't worry about the children, we'll take good care of them. They're coming here for a couple of hours tomorrow morning and I've found some old toys in the attic they'll love." Valerie didn't follow them out of the apartment, maybe she didn't want to cry in public.

"Thanks." Belle patted her mom's hand. "We're doing the right thing, aren't we?"

"Time will tell," Katrina said gruffly as they got in the car and left the town they'd briefly come to see as their home.

24

RIFT

"Do you sense anything?" They were two miles from Reggie's house. If more of Ivan's family treasure was there, Rift had hoped he'd be able to sense it by now.

Ivan shook his head. "No, all I can sense is the tiara." He sighed. "This is probably a waste of time."

"We're so close now, we might as well go all the way." Rift side-eyed his brother. "What are we going to do with the tiara?"

"I gave it to Belle." Ivan clasped his hands together and rubbed his thumbs against each other in a repetitive motion.

"She can't keep it. Not if this is the effect it has on you." Rift stared ahead. He could sense Belle as they neared Reggie's house. If this was how Ivan felt about the tiara then it would be like a nagging toothache that never goes away.

"I'll have to figure out how far away it needs to be before I can't sense it."

"How far have you tested it so far?" Rift asked.

"If it's in Wishing Moon Bay, I can sense it," Ivan replied.

"Which proves the rest of your treasure isn't there either."

Rift gnawed his lower lip. They were close to Reggie's house now, close to the place where he'd first met his mate.

"Yeah, I've thought about that. I also don't think it's on the dragon isle. I flew out over the ocean last night, just to see if I could sense anything..." Ivan turned and looked out of the window, but he soon went back to staring ahead.

"So that leaves the world beyond," Oscar mused. "It could take a while to search the whole world."

"It can stay where it is," Ivan replied. "I don't want it if it's going to mess with my head like this. I burnt the sauce I was making for dinner at the restaurant yesterday. I never burn anything."

Rift smothered his smile, but his shoulders shook as he started to laugh. "Sorry, but that's so funny."

Ivan jerked his head around to look at his brother. "I'm glad you find my pain amusing."

"I don't know many people who would love their cooking more than treasure." He sputtered as tears misted his eyes and his brother bristled next to him. "I shouldn't laugh."

Ivan shook his head and cracked a smile. "No, you should." He chuckled. "It is kind of funny, I guess." He ran his hand through his hair, his eyes crackling as he erupted into laughter. "Okay, it's a lot funny."

Oscar laughed quietly from the back seat. They'd taken the detective's car, but he'd insisted on Rift driving so that he could go through his notes once more. The backseat of the car resembled a well-organized office. Oscar's resourcefulness never ceased to amaze Rift. "I've known you boys for a long time, and I believe food has always been important to you. Why would it change now?"

Ivan leaned on the door and rested his chin on his hand. "Thank you for giving me perspective, Rift."

"You're welcome." He sensed his mate slowing down, the distance between them shorter. Belle and Katrina had arrived at Reggie's house. "Hey, can you call Katrina and check if they're all right?"

"You're worried that someone is lying in wait for them?" Ivan picked up Rift's phone and pressed dial. "Hey, Katrina. It's Ivan."

"Put it on speaker." Rift's anxiety grew even though they were only a couple of minutes behind them.

A lot can happen in a couple of minutes, his snow leopard said.

If only there weren't so many houses. There are too many people around. And some of those people might be those guys. Rift ground his molars together. He hated not being there by Belle's side.

Why would they be here? His snow leopard had a point, but it didn't soothe Rift's fears.

For the same reason Ivan wanted to come check out Reggie's house. They might think the treasure is here somewhere. Rift stared ahead, his senses locked on his mate.

"We're just parking the car," Katrina reported.

"Stay in the car." Rift leaned toward the phone as he spoke.

"There's no one here," Belle's voice gave him some comfort.

"Just in case, stay in the car." Ivan sounded more like his normal self now even though they were closing in on his treasure as well as Rift's mate.

"Okay." Belle switched off the engine and Rift listened for any sounds of danger.

"Relax." Ivan put his hand on his brother's shoulder.

"I can see the house." Relief flooded him as the house came into view. Belle's car was parked outside. Everything was fine. He let out a long breath.

"I'm not the only one who needs to let go a little," Ivan said quietly.

Rift nodded. "You can end the call, we're here." He turned off the road and pulled up next to Belle's car. "Anything?"

Ivan shook his head. "If there's anything else buried here, it's not my treasure." He cracked the door open. "But while we're here, I'd like to have a look around. If that's okay?"

Belle got out of the car and joined them. "Go for it. Although we can't go inside, we already handed the keys back to the landlord."

Ivan nodded, his eyes lingering on Belle's car. The tiara still called to him. It probably always would. Rift's sympathy for his brother increased. No matter how hard he tried, he would never be free of his treasure, it was like a curse.

Maybe it'll fade, Rift's snow leopard suggested. *When we first met Belle, our feelings were more intense, and our emotions were raw. After spending more time with her, things have calmed down. We've gotten used to it.*

We adjusted, Rift agreed. *I suspect if his treasure had always been a part of his life, Ivan would have adjusted by now, too.*

He just needs time and space. Rift's snow leopard studied their brother for a moment as he went around the side of the house, heading for the backyard. *We should stop him from doing anything rash with the tiara before he's given himself time to adjust.*

That might be out of our hands. Rift tilted his head back and sniffed the air. *Someone's been here.*

The landlord? His snow leopard prowled around the outside of Rift's mind, wanting to be free. *Or someone else?*

"Rift?" Belle put her hand on his arm as he headed after Ivan. "What's wrong? You have a crazed look in your eyes. Don't say the tiara has affected you, too."

Rift swung his head around and shook his head. "No, it's something else. A familiar scent."

His eyes narrowed as he scanned the area. There were too many people around for him to pinpoint anyone in particular with his senses. But a scent, a scent he could follow. He could follow a trail and track down whoever had been here.

Oscar's phone rang, breaking his concentration. "Hello."

"Rift, you're scaring me," Belle said quietly.

"Sorry." He snapped his attention back to his mate. "Someone's been here."

"Maybe the landlord has visited the house. He might even have brought a prospective tenant to look at the property." Katrina headed toward the house, climbing the steps where Rift and Belle had first spoken, where he'd shown his other side.

"Be careful, Mom." Belle followed after her. "There might be someone here."

"There's no one here," Rift replied. "But someone has been here." He went to her and sniffed the arm of her coat. "The smell of the guy who grabbed you still lingers on the fabric."

Belle's face paled. "And that's who's been here?"

"I think so." Rift swung around and stared out into the distance. "I'm sure they've been here recently."

"I have news." Oscar held up his phone. "I have an ID on the person in the photo."

"The one who resembles the person who grabbed me?" Belle came back down the stairs.

"The door has been forced." Katrina kept her voice low as she joined the others. "Someone has been in the house. And I don't think it was the landlord."

"Okay!" Rift put up his hand. "One thing at a time."

I can track the scent, his snow leopard told him. I can hunt down the person who was here.

We need to have all the facts first, Rift answered.

"Oscar." Belle folded her arms across her body. "Who is he?" Her eyes sparkled with tears. Belle might insist she had no emotional attachment to her father, but the news that they had identified the person who had killed him seemed to hit her hard.

"His name is Davy Westward." Oscar tapped his phone

screen and turned it toward them. "Not exactly a criminal mastermind."

Rift frowned as he leaned forward to get a better look at the information on the screen. "And this is accurate?"

Oscar nodded. "My colleague is almost one hundred percent certain. The facial recognition software matched the images. With those details, he then did a background search. Davy Westward lived a couple of miles away from where Murray was found dead."

"He's a schoolteacher?" Katrina's face paled as she stared at the man suspected of killing Murray. "Is he still alive?"

"He is." Oscar nodded and flipped his phone screen. "And this is his son. Simon Westward."

"That's the guy!" Belle covered her mouth with her hands. "That's him." She glanced at Rift. "Isn't it?"

Rift sucked in a deep breath. "It is. I'm sure."

This is the guy we can smell. He was here. His snow leopard fought for his freedom.

"Someone is moving through the trees over there." Ivan's voice at his shoulder made him jump. "Two people, if I'm not mistaken."

Rift lowered his head, his eyes unfocused as he pushed his senses out farther. "I'm going after them."

"I'll come with you," Ivan said.

"It's too dangerous." Belle grabbed hold of his arm.

"We'll be fine," Rift assured her.

"You don't know if they're armed," she replied.

"This might be our only chance to end this." Rift caught her in his arms and pulled her toward him. "We won't take any risks, I promise. Now that I've found you, I don't intend to lose you."

"Then at least take the tiara." She pulled away from him and went to the car. "If this is what they want, give it to them." She glanced sideways at Ivan. "Is that still okay?"

"Yes." Ivan grabbed hold of it, his fingers gripping it so tight the whites of his knuckles showed. Then he handed it to Rift. "Take it."

Rift nodded and took the tiara from his brother. "Wait here."

"Hang on," Oscar grabbed hold of Rift's arm. "Take the car and move in around the back of them. You can flush them out in this direction."

"I don't want them to come this way." Rift glanced at Belle and Katrina. "It's not safe."

"And we don't want them to get away." Oscar handed Rift the car keys. "Take my car. We'll get into Belle's. If we're in danger, we can just drive away." He glanced at his phone. "But I don't think we are in danger."

"They already attacked Belle once before," Rift reminded the detective. "But no one got hurt. At least none of you got hurt."

"They thought they could scare two women and children into handing over their precious treasure." Belle's face flushed red. "They never expected the guys to be there."

"I think you were an easy target. As a mother, you would give them what they wanted with no fuss because you have children to protect. They misjudged the situation. And then they ran." Oscar showed them the photo of Simon Westward again. "We don't know if they want the tiara to protect someone they love."

"He might need this for his father?" Rift could see how the situation might not be exactly how it seemed.

From both sides.

"Let's go. We don't want to lose them." Ivan jerked the car door open and got inside.

"Don't take it out on my car," Oscar called after them as Rift started the engine and pulled away sharply.

"Do you buy all that?" Ivan asked sourly.

"Oscar's right, we don't have all the facts. Maybe Simon Westward is trying to protect his own family and needs the tiara." Rift shrugged. "Or maybe they are the bad guys we think they are, and the rest is just a cover story."

"You drive, I'll keep a fix on them." Ivan half-turned to face the trees on their left as they drove away from the house.

"You should pull up a map of the area, too, so we can figure out the best route to take. We need to dump the car and go on foot. We need to cut them off and force them back toward the house." Rift put his foot down on the gas and the car sped forward.

"I plan to take them down before they get anywhere near your mate," Ivan answered.

"I was thinking the same thing." Rift pointed to a road on the left. "Do I take that one?"

"Yes." Ivan's eyes were unfocused for a moment. "They're moving toward a clearing next to the road here." He pointed at the map on his phone. "My guess is that's where their vehicle is parked."

"They're not going to make it to their vehicle." He flexed his hands on the wheel as he drove toward the clearing, his frustration growing when they got stuck behind a slow-moving car. There was no way to overtake without risking a collision with an oncoming vehicle. He'd just have to practice patience.

25

BELLE

"Are we just going to wait here?" Belle took a couple of steps toward the trees.

"Belle, we're no match for those guys." Katrina caught hold of her daughter's arm and pulled her back toward her.

"Oscar, you said that you don't think they intend to hurt anyone, right?" Belle swung around to face the detective.

"I don't think so. But that doesn't mean I'm right. For all we know, these guys might be desperate and willing to do whatever it takes to get the treasure they've been looking for." Oscar pressed his lips together, his expression grim. "I don't think we should take any risks."

"But that's exactly what Rift and Ivan are doing." Belle screwed up her mouth as she tried to figure out the best move. "When they caught up with us before, they could have really hurt me."

"You still have the bruises on your wrist from where he grabbed you," her mom reminded her.

"It could have been a lot worse." Why did she feel the need to defend them?

"Because Elise smacked him over the head with a thick branch," Katrina replied.

"I don't think that's what stopped him," Belle replied. "I'm going." She pulled free of Katrina. "If it's those guys against Rift and Ivan, they might fight. But if we're there..."

"You're hoping they will all respond to the presence of a woman," Oscar said.

"Two women. If Belle's going, I'm going, too." Katrina followed her daughter and Oscar naturally followed them both.

"I want to state for the record that I believe this is a bad idea," Oscar called out.

"Duly noted." Belle kept going although she tempered her speed so that her mom and Oscar could keep up. As she glanced over her shoulder at Oscar who diligently stuck to Katrina's side, helping her and encouraging her as they crossed a rough patch of ground, a weight lifted off her chest.

Since she was a little girl who dreamed of princesses, she'd always wished that a prince would come and sweep her mom off her feet. Perhaps Oscar was that prince. He certainly seemed attracted to Katrina and in Belle's heart, no one was too old to find love.

Belle kept running, her own love was out there somewhere, and he might need her help. Sure, he was a shifter and more than able to look after himself, in most circumstances, but these weren't most circumstances. She didn't want anyone hurt. Not Rift or Ivan, or the guys who were searching for the treasure. Not until they had the full facts.

What did a schoolteacher have to do with the death of her father? And why had they been searching for the treasure for so many years? It was worth a small fortune, but not enough to waste your whole life searching for it.

Belle reached the tree line and stopped at the trail mouth.

It split three ways and she had no idea which way to go. Staring into the trees, she wished she had shifter senses. But she couldn't hear anything, and she couldn't see any signs of movement either.

"This way." Oscar came to a halt beside Belle, Katrina's hand held firmly in his as they reached the tree line.

"Are you sure?" Belle was already moving forward, taking the trail to the left before Oscar answered.

"Positive. These twigs have been broken recently and there's a fresh boot print right there." Oscar pointed to the ground as they brushed through the undergrowth, heading deeper into the trees.

"Will you teach me how to track?" Belle asked. "I might never have shifter senses, but I can learn other ways to use the senses I have."

"I'd be honored." Oscar's cheeks flushed pink with pleasure before he refocused on the trail ahead. "Watch your step."

Belle sidestepped around a loose log and jogged on along the trail. She had to switch her attention between looking at the ground immediately in front of her and the trees up ahead.

"Belle," Oscar hissed.

She slowed down and waited for her mom and Oscar to catch up. "What's wrong?"

"I thought I heard something." Oscar was breathing heavily and sweat formed on his brow. Still clutching his hand, Katrina leaned against a tree and calmed her breathing.

"What did you hear?" Belle turned to stare deeper into the trees.

"Something...or someone is coming our way." Oscar jerked his head up. "There."

"I can't see anything." She followed the direction in which he pointed.

"We should move." He reached for her and pulled her back along the trail.

"I thought we were going to help?" Belle didn't pull away from Oscar. The guy had much more experience at this kind of thing.

"We are. But we're going in blind." He parted the bushes on the side of the trail and held them apart so that Katrina and Belle could squeeze into the gap.

"We're hiding?" Katrina asked.

"Isn't that what an ambush is?" Oscar hurried along the trail about ten feet and grabbed hold of a thick branch. "You saw how Elise used it?"

A small smile spread across Belle's face. "I did."

"If they come this way, you use this to slow them down." He held up his hands and added a word of caution, "Don't hurt them too badly. We're not trying to maim or kill them."

"We're just trying to slow them down." Belle nodded her understanding. "I was never good at baseball."

"What are you going to do, Oscar?" Katrina caught hold of his arm. "I don't want you to get hurt. This isn't your fight."

"It is." Oscar patted her hand. "And I can take care of myself, don't worry."

"Take care, Oscar." Belle grasped the branch and held it up, ready to hit anyone or anything that came their way. Rift was certain the guys weren't shifters but there were other things they could be, and she didn't intend to take any chances.

"Okay. Stay alert." With that, he slipped away, and the bushes closed in around them.

"We should have stayed in the car." Katrina wrapped her arms around her body.

"Mom, it'll be okay."

Katrina nodded. "I hope so. I just can't help thinking of all the people who have been dragged into this. Good people are in danger because of the actions of two bad men."

"It's not your fault. It never was."

"I chose your father. I was so naive. So stupid." She brushed her hand over her eyes and then took a deep breath. "I should have a weapon, too."

Belle ducked down and looked around on the ground at her feet, there was little room to move but she spotted a short thick tree branch that she might be able to reach. "Here, hold this and keep a lookout," she whispered to her mom.

Katrina nodded and curled her fingers around the tree branch Oscar had found. With one last look along the trail to check that no one was coming, she ducked down and scrambled under the bush to reach the stick. Stretching out her arm, she managed to touch the branch with the tips of her fingers. Forcing her shoulder forward into the bush, she stretched farther and at last grabbed the branch.

"Here." She passed the short branch to her mom.

"Thanks." Katrina froze and then pointed to the trail.

Someone was coming.

A flash of movement and a magnificent snow leopard appeared on the trail. Rift.

For a second, everything else slipped away. He was the most incredible thing she'd ever seen and when he turned and looked straight at her, it was as if they were frozen in a moment of time.

Then the world exploded as he leaped forward, crashing into a guy who ran around the corner, right into the snow leopard's path.

Belle broke cover and ran forward, the branch raised as she went to the aid of her mate. Not that he needed it, he seemed to be handling the situation without maiming the other guy.

Another shout drew her attention. Oscar was fighting with a second man. He was severely outmatched by the younger man. Belle ran forward, the branch raised ready to strike as she recognized the man. Simon Westward.

"Stop!" she yelled, her voice weak and small to her ears but it was enough to stop the two men. "We have what you want."

Oscar stepped back as Simon froze, his gaze fixed on Belle. "You lied to us, we knew it."

She shook her head. "No, I didn't have it then. I didn't know what you were talking about."

"But you have it now?" His eyes were hungry as she nodded.

Rift's snow leopard snarled, a low threatening growl emanating from him. "Tell him to stop fighting." She pointed back along the trail.

"And then what?" Simon asked.

"You take your treasure and leave. Just like that." A nagging voice in her head told her they needed an explanation. Ivan needed an explanation.

"Okay." Simon nodded, the deal was done. Would Ivan be okay with it? Or would he track these men down and take back what was his?

"Ivan." The dragon shifter ran along the trail toward them. Would he keep to the deal?

Ivan slid to a stop ten feet away from them, his eyes fixed on Rift, who shifted back to his human form, the tiara in his hand. "Go ahead."

"Are you sure?" Belle asked. She didn't want bloodshed if Rift passed the tiara to Simon and Ivan changed his mind and made a grab for it.

"Positive." As he nodded, the other guy came toward them. Behind him, Rift ran to help Katrina.

"Okay then." She inhaled deeply. She could sense Ivan

getting closer, like a moth drawn to a flame. Was this the right thing to do? Why should they hand over such a priceless item to a stranger without even knowing his claim to it?

But this was the deal she'd made. If it kept her and her family safe, surely it was the right thing to do? As Rift and Katrina joined them, her resolved firmed. It was just a piece of jewelry.

Although, as Rift handed it to her and she weighed it in her hands, it was as if heat flared where the jewels touched her skin. It was as if it were alive.

Which was impossible.

"Here." She held out the tiara and lifted her gaze to meet Simon's.

"What is that?" He jabbed his finger at the tiara.

"This is the treasure you wanted." Belle glanced over her shoulder at Ivan. Had he switched it for a similar piece? She rubbed her thumb over the sapphire embedded in the tiara. It looked the same to her, but she was no expert.

"That isn't it." Simon closed the distance between them, and Ivan bristled, moving rapidly to her side. Did he sense danger from Simon, who obviously thought she was trying to fool him?

"This is the only treasure we found at the house." Her forehead creased as she held it out to him. "Take it."

"No, it's not the right piece." He half-turned and looked at his friend who came to join them. "This isn't it."

"Let me see." The guy looked over Simon's shoulder and took a sharp breath. "Damn it!"

"Then we don't have what you want," Belle said firmly and turned to Ivan. "Thanks, Ivan. It looks as if you can have this back."

Ivan hesitated before he reached for it, his eyes glowing amber as his skin came into contact with the jewels. "Thank you."

"We're done here," Belle told Simon. "We don't have what you want..."

"You're a dragon shifter?" Simon completely ignored Belle as he stared at Ivan.

Ivan lifted his head and looked at Simon. "As Belle said, we're done here." His jaw tightened.

"My father knew a dragon shifter," Simon continued.

"Did he?" Ivan's eyes glowed brighter, their color deepening.

"The dragon shifter was murdered." Simon licked his lips nervously. "The treasure I seek will prove who killed him. It'll also prove who killed your father." He turned to face Belle.

"From the information the police have, we believe your father was responsible for killing my father," Belle said shortly, tired of this charade.

"Which is why I'm here," Simon replied. "When Reginald was released from prison, we thought we'd finally be able to clear my father's name."

"Your father was never arrested or sent to trial for the murder of Murray." Oscar joined the conversation but didn't move from Katrina's side.

"No, but he saw the photo. He's lived his whole life knowing that one day someone might link it to him. He's a recluse, it ruined his life," Simon replied.

"So why didn't he come forward and clear his name before?" Oscar asked.

"Because he was set up and the only proof he had was a piece of jewelry. A pendant that the real killer gave to Murray as payment for tracking down the dragon shifter. This shifter then killed Murray. He intended to take back his treasure and cover his tracks. But he never recovered the treasure and since my father was implicated in Murray's murder, he thought he was safe."

"Who was safe?" Oscar asked. "You know who was responsible? I can help you clear your father's name and bring the person to justice."

Simon laughed and shook his head. "I'm sure you think you can, but you have no idea who you are dealing with. The pendant is the only thing that can prove who did this and bring him down."

"What did the pendant look like?" Katrina asked.

"A large teardrop diamond." The second guy spun around to look at Belle's mom.

Instinctively, Belle moved to put herself between the guy and her mom, but Oscar moved, too. Despite the difference in size, Oscar would defend Katrina, it was there in his eyes.

"Belle." Katrina switched her attention to her daughter. "Do you remember that pendant you used to like to wear when you played dress up?"

"Oh, my!" Belle covered her mouth with her hands. "It was a real diamond?"

"You have it?" Simon's face paled and he stumbled forward.

Rift instantly sprang forward his hand on Simon's chest. "Back off, buddy."

"It's okay." Belle's shoulders sagged as she cupped her face in her hands. "I think I know where it is."

"You think..." Simon's voice trailed off as Rift rumbled a warning. "Please, it's important to me."

"We should go to my house," Belle replied. "I had it in the drawer of my nightstand. I was going to let Rosie have it to go with her princess dresses, but it was the only thing I had that belonged to my dad."

"Murray gave it to me a couple of weeks before he died. I thought it was fake, a lump of shiny glass," Katrina confessed. "I gave it to Belle to play with."

"Can we go now?" Simon asked.

Belle nodded. "It's more important to you than me."

She just hoped it was where she'd left it. If not, it might be lost forever.

26

RIFT

Rift pulled onto the driveway behind Belle's car and switched off the engine before he glanced in the rearview mirror. "And we're sure we can trust these guys?"

"I think so. If they were just after the pendant because it was of value, then they would have taken the tiara. They didn't." Oscar glanced at Ivan who had been silent during most of the trip.

"They were talking about my father, weren't they?" Ivan finally asked.

"I believe so."

"He was murdered by another dragon shifter." Ivan locked eyes with Oscar. "Did you know?"

"No. I had no idea." Oscar turned to face Ivan. "This pendant isn't just important to these guys. It's also the key to your past and maybe your future."

"My future." Ivan's jaw clenched. "My future lies at the hotel. With my family."

"You don't want to find out more about your father? You have a chance right now. You could go meet Davy Westward.

He personally knew your father. He could tell you what kind of a person he was. He could also tell you why he was killed. And who by."

"And spend the rest of my life searching for revenge? Being caught up in the past like Simon Westward and his family." Ivan reached for the door handle and cranked it open.

"Ivan." Rift turned in his seat and caught hold of his brother's arm. "Think about it. At least go talk to Davy Westward. I'd give anything to know more about my parents. You have that chance."

Ivan avoided Rift's eyes as he nodded. "I'll think about it." With that he got out of the car and stalked toward the road, his hands shoved in his pockets as he looked right and left, waiting for the others to arrive.

"He needs time," Oscar said quietly. "He has decisions to make. Hard decisions."

"If only the kids hadn't found the tiara," Rift murmured.

"No, it's a good thing. The Westward family needs closure. And as for Ivan..." Oscar glanced in the mirror. "Maybe your brother's life is just about to open up."

"Whether he wants it to or not?" Rift asked.

"Life has a way of doing just that," Oscar answered.

"Is that the voice of experience?" Rift placed his hand on the car door, ready to open it.

"That is the voice of a man whose own life seems about to open up in a surprising and unexpected way." Oscar's eyes were drawn to Katrina who was approaching the car.

"Grab ahold of it with both hands, Oscar. You deserve happiness and so does Katrina." He placed his hand on the older man's back. "Don't waste a second."

"I won't." Oscar took a long breath. "It's scary, though."

"It's a good thing you're such a brave man." Rift opened the car door and got out. "How are you doing, Katrina?"

"Shaken up. It's all a shock." She hugged herself as she stood by the side of the car. "Belle's gone inside to look for the pendant. I don't think I can stand the suspense."

Rift glanced toward the front door of Belle's house. Situated in the suburbs, it was a nondescript family home, the kind he'd have driven past without a second glance, never knowing his mate was inside. Yet he could sense her.

He looked up toward the front bedroom window as if he could see through the walls of the house. But his senses weren't that good.

"She's coming." He held his breath as Belle left the bedroom and came running downstairs.

"She's found it!" Katrina ran back toward the house and Oscar got out of the car and followed.

"Belle." Rift met his mate at the front door.

"This is it." She held up pendant. "It just doesn't look real."

Oscar reached out and cupped the dangling diamond in his hand. "Ask Ivan."

"How would Ivan know?" Rift asked.

"Dragons know these things, believe me." He inclined his head toward Ivan who was still loitering on the sidewalk.

"Ivan." Rift took Belle's hand and they hurried toward his brother.

"Do you have it?" Ivan swung around to face them, his eyes widening as he saw the diamond pendant. "You thought that was a glass bauble?"

Belle shrugged. "I did. I get the feeling I was wrong."

Ivan stepped closer, as he did, a car drove up and parked across the street. Simon Westward got out along with the other guy and came toward them. "It's real." Ivan held out his hand but didn't touch the gem. "I can sense it. It has an aura." His hand snapped back to his side. "Fiona showed me some of her treasure. It has a different aura. She said all treasure is unique to its owner. Like it's part of them."

"Like the tiara is part of you." Belle nodded in understanding. "And you were willing to give it up for us."

"You are family and family are more important than any treasure." Ivan backed away as the other men approached.

"Here. This is what you came for." Belle thrust her hand out to them.

"You're just going to hand it over?" Simon Westward asked.

"Yes. It's not mine. And if I kept it or sold it, I'd feel like I had blood on my hands." She let it drop into Simon's palm. "Take it. I just want your word that we're done here. Neither me nor my mom had anything to do with what happened. My mom left my father months before any of this occurred."

"We couldn't be sure that you knew about this." Simon closed his hand around the pendant. "I'm sorry we scared you."

Belle's eyes narrowed. "I understand why you did it. But if you threaten my family again in any way..."

"We won't." Simon glanced at Ivan. "My father would like to meet you."

"I'll think about it," Ivan replied.

"We could go now. My mom is cooking dinner. There's always room at the table for one more." Simon stepped backward, his eagerness to get home and show his father the pendant evident.

"Go." Rift patted Ivan on the back. "You'll regret it if you don't."

Ivan stared at the ground for a moment and then nodded. "I'll make my own way home. I plan to go visit Fiona for a couple of days since Elise is running the kitchen."

"Take your time," Rift replied.

"I will." Ivan nodded.

"Call Zara and Karros. They can come pick you up and take you back to Bear Creek," Rift told him.

Ivan nodded. "I might do that. Or I might fly. I need to stretch my wings and sort through my thoughts."

"Just take care of yourself." Rift pulled Ivan into a tight hug. "And remember where your family is."

"I'll never forget where you are," Ivan assured him. "It's just when I come back home, I need to be whole again. Right now I feel as if I'm torn in two. Like there are two halves of me and I need to figure out how they go back together."

"Take your time." Rift held onto his brother, not wanting to let him go. There had to be a way to help him.

He needs time, Rift's snow leopard said. He needs time and space.

There's time and space in Wishing Moon Bay, Rift replied.

There's time but not space, his snow leopard answered. We're all so concerned about him that there's a danger we might suffocate him.

"If you need me, just call." Ivan nodded and then turned and walked away.

"Hey…" Belle threaded her fingers through his. "If you need to go with him, it's okay. We'll be okay. Oscar can show us the way back to Wishing Moon Bay."

"No." He shook his head and turned to face her, cupping her cheek in his hand. "I think this is one thing Ivan needs to do on his own. We're his family, he knows that but for once we're not what he needs."

"He needs to spread his wings," Oscar's attempt to lift the mood didn't help. "Sorry. I'm just relieved that this is over for you both. And that Rift and Belle can start making plans for the future."

"There's still a lot of questions we don't have answers to," Katrina said.

"Do we really need those answers?" Belle asked. "Sure, Ivan needs to know what happened and so do Caleb and Aiden. But the answers are to questions I never asked. My dad died before I ever knew him." She stepped closer to her mom and put her arm around her shoulders. "And you let go of him years ago. Don't let him spoil your future."

"My future?" Katrina glanced at her daughter and then turned away, her cheeks pink as heat crept across her skin.

Belle wants her mom to give Oscar a chance, Rift's snow leopard said. Do you think she will?

I do. Rift covered his smile.

"Shall we go have some coffee?" Belle pulled Rift toward the house.

"I am going to go check on my apartment," Katrina replied. "Do you want to come, Oscar? I'll treat you to dinner."

"Yes," Oscar blurted out before he composed himself. "Although, I'm an old-fashioned guy and would prefer dinner to be my treat."

"We can discuss it on the way," Katrina replied. "You two should have some time alone."

"Subtle, Mom." Belle squeezed Rift's hand as she grinned.

"Shall we meet back here tomorrow morning?" Katrina asked. "It's too late to drive back tonight and we're all tired. I have a guest room, Oscar. Unless you need to go back to Wishing Moon Bay tonight."

"No. Tomorrow morning is fine with me. Perhaps if you insist on buying dinner, I could buy us breakfast." Oscar and Katrina headed for the car, looking like an old married couple.

"They look great together." Belle leaned on Rift's shoulder.

"They look happy together." Rift put his arm around her. "Shall we go get that coffee? You look tired."

"Thanks." She screwed her face up. "You might need to work on your compliments."

Rift chuckled. "That was me showing my concern. It's been a long and stressful day."

"You can say that again. I was so worried that the pendant wasn't here. I nearly let Rosie have it for her dress-up box a couple of months ago." Belle went into the house and closed the door behind Rift.

"Why didn't you?"

She shrugged. "Because it was the only link I had to my father." Her eyes misted with tears. "I know what I said about not wanting to know anything about him and not needing to know the answers to all the questions surrounding him and what he did."

"But he was still your dad." Rift nodded in understanding.

"He was. I used to lie awake at night and dream of what it would be like to have a dad." She arched her eyebrow. "The kind of dad my friends had. One who went out to work and came home each evening. Not the kind who does bad things."

"There's times I did the same. Valerie was the best mom in the world but seeing my friends with their fathers…"

"Which is what made it so much harder when Landon left. I don't want Rosie and Jack growing up not having a father." She put the coffee on and then turned to face him. "Which is why I am willing to throw myself into this relationship with you."

"Throw yourself." He held out his arms, his expression serious. "I'm here to catch you. Always."

"I didn't believe in shifters until you showed me your snow leopard. I didn't believe in mates either but now I think I do." She went to him and wrapped her arms around him. "And now I believe in love, too. Because I feel it in my heart."

Rift held his breath as he tightened his arms around her. "Love is all that matters, Belle. Love for friends and family, it's more precious than any jewel."

"I want to make love right now." Her words blindsided

him and he stared at her for a long moment as if he hadn't comprehended what she'd said.

"We don't have to rush." Was he really trying to persuade her not to go to bed with him? He must be crazy, he'd craved her since the moment they met. Yet he didn't want her to have regrets. Today had been a traumatic day and people made bad choices when they were in a highly emotional state.

"So that's a no?" She arched an eyebrow as she watched his expression.

"Oh, I want to." He put his hand over his heart. "I meant…"

"It's what I want." She placed her hand over his as it rested on his chest. "I want you."

"Bedroom?" He could barely get the word out, it was as if she'd knocked the wind out of him.

She pointed upwards as heat flared across her skin. Rift wanted to strip off her clothes and chase that heat. But not here in the kitchen. What if her mom came back to check on them or something?

His snow leopard chuckled. That would be embarrassing.

Rift scooped her up into his arms and cradled her against his chest as he headed for the stairs. He forced himself to slow down and take the stairs one at a time even though he could barely control his need to claim his mate.

"Which room?" he growled.

Belle pointed to the second door on the right and he pushed the door open with his hip before going inside.

The room was painted a pale cream with floral drapes and a hand-carved wooden bedframe covered in a matching bedspread. It was a pretty, functional room and he suspected the curtains and bedding were new, perhaps Belle had wanted to transform the room after Landon left.

He lay her on the bed, the same bed she'd probably shared

with her husband for so many years. He hovered over her and lowered his head, pressing his lips to hers as he cupped her breast in his hand and rubbed his thumb over her nipple.

She groaned and arched her back as if offering herself to him. Rift slid his hand between her thighs. She gasped as he touched her through the fabric of her jeans and opened her thighs wider. With each stroke of his fingers, her arousal intensified, and her nipples hardened into taut buds as he teased them.

Belle covered his hand with hers, her lips parted as she moaned softly, craving his attention.

"Are you sure?" he whispered against her ear.

She turned her head, nuzzling his neck, sending thrills through his body. "Yes." She placed her hand over his groin and stroked his hard length, as if reinforcing her answer.

Rift hooked his fingers into the waistband of her jeans and pushed them down over her hips. Hiding her embarrassment, she let her hair fall over her face as she murmured, "It's been a long time since I was naked in front of anyone but..."

"We'll take it slow," Rift reassured her as he reached down and helped her wriggle out of her jeans.

"I don't know if I want to take it slow." She tugged at the hem of his shirt and pulled it up over his head. Casting it aside, she lifted her head off the bed and pressed her lips to his tanned skin, her tongue curling around his nipple as she worked to unbuckle his belt.

"I'm here for you, whatever you want." Rift's breath hissed through his teeth as she finally unbuttoned his jeans and pushed them down over his hips, before curling her hand around his hard length.

"I want you." She sat up and quickly peeled off her shirt and bra before diving under the covers.

"Is there room in there for me?" He left his jeans pooled

on the bedroom floor and climbed, naked, into the bed beside her.

"I think I can squeeze you in." She shuffled across the bed and he snuggled next to her, his hand around her waist as he pulled her close. "A perfect fit."

Rift cupped her cheek in his hand and stared down at her for a long moment before he leaned forward and brushed his lips across hers. He savored the taste of her, she was so unique, so his.

Belle stroked his chest, her fingers trailing down over his stomach and lower.

Rift closed his eyes as she curled her fingers around his hardness and stroked him, with just the right amount of pressure. He bit down on his lower lip as he fought for control, which was almost impossible. They were meant to be together, joined as one.

Licking his lips, he lowered his head and sucked in her hardened nipple, teasing her with his tongue. Swirling it around and around, he regained his senses and cupped her breast in his hand, massaging her sensitive flesh.

She groaned and writhed on the bed, parting her thighs and inviting him to lie between them. As if they were caught up in their own private dance, where only they knew the steps and the rhythm, he moved to nestle between her thighs, guiding himself into her.

She tensed, her back arched before she let out a long-contented sigh and relaxed. Rift thrust forward, entering her and reveling in the feel of her surrounding him. Belle nipped his neck, driving his arousal higher and he slid his hand underneath her, holding her to him as he lunged forward, filling her completely.

Rift pulled back before thrusting his hips forward and sensations flooded his body. He was so close to coming but he wanted this to last longer. The touch of his mate, the feel of her surrounding him, stroking him, kissing him was something he wanted to prolong for hours.

But he couldn't keep in control for that long. She overwhelmed him.

Rift moved with a steady rhythm as he took her with him to new heights. They moved as one, two bodies joined as they raced toward their climax.

When he finally came, he rocked his hips, moving slowly inside her while her inner muscles tightened and milked his essence from him. Belle cried out, her fingernails raking his skin and he captured her mouth, kissing her until they were completely sated.

As they lay in each other's arms, exhaustion crept up on them and they slept. Together at last with no worries about what might be lurking outside.

27

BELLE

Belle stared out of the window at the early morning sun. She'd watched the sun rise from the kitchen window countless times. On days when she'd been up with the children all night when they'd suffered from coughs and colds and other childhood illnesses.

She'd watched the sun rise after sleepless nights when her mind wouldn't switch off as it tried to figure out where her marriage had gone wrong and how she was going to cope alone.

This morning she'd watched the sun rise with her heart filled with love for the man who called her mate. The man she was willing to uproot her life for.

Belle raked her hand through her hair. She must be crazy. With a good job and the children settled in their schools, her plans to move to Wishing Moon Bay were an act of madness.

"Morning." Rift entered the kitchen, she'd have to get used to him moving around so quietly.

Yes, she would. A small smile crept over her face as he wrapped his arms around her waist and nuzzled her neck.

Belle lifted her arms and encircled his neck, turning her face as she pressed her lips against his cheek.

"Morning. I thought you were still asleep."

"The bed got cold without you in it." He inhaled deeply and looked out of the kitchen window. "I want to spend every sunrise with you."

Belle turned around, her back to the window. "I'd like that." She put the heel of her hand to her forehead. "Which sounds absolutely crazy."

He tilted his head to one side and looked at her sideways. "It's good to be a little crazy sometimes."

"I've worked so hard to keep it all together." Tears pricked her eyes and she looked away from him, not wanting him to see her cry. She didn't want him to think she was weak.

"Just because you move to Wishing Moon Bay and make a new start doesn't mean you are giving up." He stroked her cheek, his fingertips spreading heat in their wake. "Opening your heart when you've been hurt is a brave thing to do."

"I just worry if it's the right thing for the children. Taking them away from their school and their friends." Belle had always wanted to give them stability. It was even more important after their father left. For weeks, Rosie had asked if Landon was coming to read her a bedtime story. As for Jack, Belle would be forever haunted by her son's eyes searching for his father as he stood shoulder to shoulder with his teammates.

"Take your time. There's no rush." He held her tightly and soothed her, his voice warm and low.

She rested her head on his shoulder. "I'm just scared of making another mistake."

"Hey." He put his hands on her upper arms and held her away from him. "If you think you are to blame for their dad walking out, you're not. It was his choice. I don't know the reasons for your breakup, but I do know that they are his children, and he shouldn't have just abandoned them. That is entirely on him."

Belle nodded. Here was a man who would never leave her. They were mates.

"Okay." She nodded. "A fresh start in a new town would be a good way of putting all of this behind us. We can move on together. The four of us."

He cocked his head on one side and smiled. "Or five or six." His smile widened. "Do you want more children?"

She closed the space between them and cupped his face in her hands. "I wouldn't object if we were blessed with a brother or sister for Rosie and Jack. I always wanted a bigger family since mine was so small. It was only ever me and my mom. I didn't want my kids to feel as if they were alone."

"There's a big family waiting for them in Wishing Moon Bay. I know it'll make everyone happy to have you all living there." He leaned his forehead against hers. "I wish I could go back and make things easier for you as a child."

"My mom did her best. It's not as if I'm traumatized. I never had a dad to miss." She gave a small, humorless laugh. "Yet it still affected me. I don't want my kids to grow up like that."

"All you can do is be there for them." Rift sucked in a shuddering breath. "I never had a father either. But I want to be a father to your children. I'm going to make mistakes. I'm hoping your children will be patient with me and teach me as much as I teach them. Family is all about learning from each other."

She tilted her head back and captured his lips, their kiss deepening as he tightened his arms around her. He nipped her lower lip, and she opened her mouth as tendrils of desire unfurled in her belly. Perhaps she should drag him back to bed.

But her mom and Oscar would be here in a couple of

hours and she wanted to pack the things they needed to take back with them. She planned to spend a few days with Rift, figuring out how they were going to make the move work before she came back here and started to pack up her life.

"Coffee's ready." Belle didn't break away from Rift, she liked him holding her. It wasn't just that he made her feel safe, now that the threat from Simon Westward had passed, there was nothing to be afraid of.

Until Rift, she hadn't realized how much she'd missed the touch of a lover's embrace. She thought she could live without it, and she would have. Perhaps, because she'd never experienced the same kind of connection with anyone else.

Now, the touch of his fingers on her skin, the warmth of his body next to hers, were something she never wanted to be without. Not for one day.

It was as if the mating bond between them worked both ways. It wasn't only Rift and his shifter side that experienced the connection.

A thrill of excitement coursed through her. This was real. More real than anything she'd ever experienced before. It was as if a part of her that had always been dormant was now awakened.

Her life was about to start anew. It went deeper than a new house in a new town. This was a new Belle.

"Coffee would be great." Rift didn't relinquish his hold on her either. He stared down at her. "Maybe we could get the cups and pour the coffee while still holding onto each other because I really don't want to let you go."

She took hold of his hand and lifted it, pressing it to her lips. "I need both my hands so I can pack."

He sighed. "In that case, you go start packing while I make coffee. Do you want breakfast, too?"

"I do. There are some eggs and bacon." She waved her hand at him. "Just help yourself to whatever you can find."

"I'm not as good at cooking as Ivan, but I can make breakfast." He leaned over and kissed her cheek as she headed out of the kitchen.

"I can't wait to eat. Since we kind of skipped dinner last night." Her cheeks flamed red as she left the kitchen with thoughts of their night together in her mind.

Okay, it was time to get her head straight and figure out what they would need for a few days in Wishing Moon Bay. Belle also figured she might take some stuff to leave there, like a few changes of clothes and some toys and games. They might need to visit the town a few times before they actually moved there. It would be great to not have to pack each time.

She went to her closet and pulled down the large suitcase they used for vacations. Flipping it open, she went to the children's rooms and grabbed some clothes before rummaging through the toybox. After ten minutes, she'd half-filled the case and began adding her things. She also added spare toothbrushes and some other personal items.

"Hey, breakfast is ready." Rift came into the room, she hadn't heard him walk up the stairs.

"Thanks." She sat down on the bed and flipped the case shut. "It seems weird to think we're going to leave this house."

"Have you lived here for long?" Rift came to sit next to her and reached for her hand.

"Yes. We bought it when I got my promotion at work before the children came along." She swallowed the lump of emotion in her throat and fought back tears. "I always thought Landon and I would raise the children and grow old together here."

"Do you still love him?" Rift didn't look at her as he asked the question.

"No." She shook her head firmly. "He might have been the one that left but I knew our relationship had lost its sparkle for months before it happened. I tried talking to him about it. I even suggested we go to counseling, but he wasn't interested. Of course, I now know it's because he had a secret life with another woman. But over those weeks and months, the love I had for him shriveled up. It got smaller and smaller. When he left, it died."

"I needed to hear that." Rift half turned to face her. "I'm sorry you got hurt."

"Not your fault." Her mouth curved up at one corner.

"I'm going to work hard to make sure we never lose our sparkle." He slipped his arm around her shoulder and she leaned into him.

"We're a team. You and me. Us and the kids. As long as we always remember that and are open about our feelings, we'll do just fine." Belle placed her hand on his thigh and squeezed it lightly. "I am in love with you, Rift, and I plan to keep that love alive for the rest of my life."

"I love you, too, Belle." He chuckled as his stomach rumbled. "Come on, let's go eat before we move on with the rest of our lives together."

He pulled her to her feet, and she wrapped her arms around his neck, her lips grazing his before they left the room. In the doorway, she turned and looked back at the bed where her children had been conceived. But all memories of Landon were gone, replaced by Rift.

Fate had brought them together and she was going to make sure nothing tore them apart.

EPILOGUE

"You look nice." Belle stirred the pasta sauce as Katrina came into the kitchen.

"You don't think it's too much?" Katrina smoothed her hands over her purple skirt that she'd paired with a cream blouse and a pale mauve cardigan.

"I think it's perfect." Belle turned down the stove and wiped her hands as she approached her mom. "And I think Oscar is perfect, too."

Katrina blushed, her cheeks tinged with pink as she smothered a smile. "I didn't think I'd ever fall for a man again. But Oscar is so kind and such good company."

"You two are great together." Belle hugged her mom, holding her tight as she fought back tears of happiness. "We're so incredibly lucky."

Katrina buried her face in Belle's shoulder and sucked in a shuddering breath. "I was thinking about it while I got dressed. How after everything Reggie did, all the bad stuff, if it wasn't for him being my brother, we would never have wound up here in Wishing Moon Bay."

"Are you happy we moved?" Belle and her family had

finally moved to Wishing Moon Bay two weeks ago. Preparing for the move had been emotionally and physically exhausting. However, the first night in their new house, which Rift had bought for them all to live in, had felt as if they had come home. There was no other way she could describe it.

"This is the best thing we've ever done." Katrina lifted her head and glanced out of the kitchen window. "And the kids are so happy."

Belle slid her arm around her mom's shoulder as she turned to look out of the window, too. Rosie and Jack were helping Rift build a treehouse in the backyard that backed onto a small, wooded area which in turn led to a trail that led straight into the mountains.

Perfect for a snow leopard to go for a run whenever he wanted. Plus, it was ideal for hiking with two young children. Belle was also getting used to the idea that Rosie and Jack could go exploring on their own if Rift was home. They had a sense of freedom even though Rift could keep tabs on them at all times.

"And we're happy." Belle smiled down at her mom. "I don't think I say it enough, but I love you, Mom."

"I love you, too, Belle. And I'm so very proud of you."

"We did okay, didn't we?" Belle grinned broadly.

There was only one nagging worry in her mind. Rift didn't speak of it often, but she knew he was worried about Ivan. Reggie might have brought Belle and Katrina to Wishing Moon Bay. But his actions had also cause Ivan pain, pain that he tried to hide.

She only hoped he might one day heal. Perhaps if he too found his mate, that healing might begin.

If only finding a mate was that simple.

THANKS FOR READING!

I hope you enjoyed my book!

The next book in this series is 'The Dragon Shifter's Desire', which you can find on my website: harmonyraines.com/all-books/bond-of-brothers-series

If you'd like to keep up with my new releases, and any offers, you can follow me on Facebook at:

facebook.com/harmonyrainesauthor

Or you can head over to my website and sign up to my newsletter for notifications about releases and exclusive deals.

Feel free to message me on Facebook, or send an email to harmony@harmonyraines.com.

Harmony.

THE DRAGON SHIFTER'S DESIRE

THE BOND OF BROTHERS - BOOK SIX

Get it here:
US: amazon.com/dp/B09CLMFDMF
UK: amazon.co.uk/dp/B09CLMFDMF

LARISA

"How's Dad?" Larisa asked her brother, Simon, as he met her in the driveway of the home they'd both grown up in. She'd been away for a couple of months, traveling to the Himalayas after she'd heard a rumor that dragons had been spotted flying over the mountains.

She'd found nothing. Although, she believed the rumors were true. The local people had simply chosen to keep the secret of the mythical winged beasts.

Larisa had worked to gain the trust of the people in a remote mountain village, and she was certain they were about to open up to her when Simon called and summoned her home.

"He's...agitated." Simon strode toward her, worry etched into his face as he flung his arms around her shoulders and pulled her into his arms. "I've missed you, Larisa."

She grabbed hold of him, her fingers digging into his sweater as she clung to him. "I missed you, too."

They were bound together by the deep love they shared for their father, who had raised them alone, and the desire to free him from the chains of depression that had gripped him tightly for decades.

"Are you sure you found it?" She held him for one moment longer, comforted by the familiarity of the person she trusted most in the world. Simon always had her back. Just as Larisa always had his.

"Yes." He stepped away and stared at the ground, unable to look her in the eye.

She let out a long breath and tears pricked her eyes. "Okay then."

He gave a short laugh. "It's anything but *okay*."

"That's better." She punched him in the arm. "We'll figure it out. One step at a time, right? This is the breakthrough we've been searching for."

"There's more." He glanced toward the house. "I couldn't tell you on the phone."

Ice crept up her spine. "Tell me what?" Had her father's health taken a downturn since they'd finally made a breakthrough?

"Not here either." He nodded toward the house. "Dad's taking a nap. Let's go around the back and grab some coffee." He glanced sideways at her. "You look well. The mountain air suited you."

"It was so beautiful. So serene even though the village only had basic amenities." She inhaled deeply, missing the cool crisp mountain air she'd grown to love.

"I'm sorry I called you back." His forehead creased and sorrow crept into his eyes.

"Simon, I came because this is what we've both been working for." She slid her arm around his shoulders as they headed toward the house. "Finding the pendant is huge. It's the breakthrough we've been searching for."

Simon nodded and they headed around the side of the house without talking. Their father, Davy Westward, had always had trouble sleeping. He was haunted by dreams that he never spoke of. Although, over the years, Larisa and Simon had pieced together the puzzle of what haunted him.

Simon opened the kitchen door, and they went inside. Larisa dumped her pack by the door and closed it quietly while Simon poured coffee and grabbed a package of cookies from the cupboard. Larisa left the kitchen and tiptoed down the hallway, peeking inside the living room to check on her father who snored lightly as he slept in his old recliner chair.

Her mouth turned down at the corners. He looked so old, his face crumpled and tense even in sleep. She swallowed hard, this was no time to cry. This was time to fight.

"So what's your other news?" She pulled out a chair and sat down at the kitchen table and picked up a cookie. Taking a bite, she closed her eyes and savored the sugar rush. "I've missed junk food."

"I've missed you," Simon said with a cheesy grin.

"Don't change the subject. I need to hear your news." She tilted her head to one side trying to read his expression. "Is it good or bad?"

"Good." He sighed and slumped back in his chair, running his hand over the surface of the table as he kept his eyes downcast. "I guess."

"Are you trying to kill me with the suspense?" She finished her cookie and lifted her cup of coffee to her lips.

"No." His forehead crumpled, the creases deep, as if he shouldered the weight of the world.

"Simon."

"I told you how we found the pendant."

"You said you got it from Murray's daughter. That she had it all these years." Her shoulders tensed as she fought off the feeling of failure that settled on her. It was right there all this time. Not even hidden away in a bank vault. She shook off her sense of failure, it was no use to her now. She needed to direct her energy toward the future and the next step they had to take.

"What I didn't tell you was that Murray's daughter, Belle, is the mate of a shifter, Rift." Simon's jaw tensed and he swallowed hard.

"What kind of shifter?" Larisa held her breath as her brother sipped his coffee. The suspense truly was going to kill her.

"A snow leopard."

Her breath left her in one long exhale, and she gave a short laugh. "I thought you were going to say a dragon shifter."

"No, that would be Rift's brother, Ivan." He met her eyes and held it as a myriad of emotions coursed through her. Disbelief, followed by shock, followed by suspicion.

"How do you know?" Her eyes widened. "Did you see him?" Ever since her father told them that dragon shifters were real, they'd dreamed of seeing one in the flesh. There were nights when she'd lie in bed, unable to sleep as her head filled with images of great winged beasts that ruled the sky, she'd often question her reasons for searching the world for one.

Was it purely because she wanted to help her father or was it because of her selfish desire to see one with her own eyes?

Perhaps those two reasons were entwined together. One led to the other. If she saw one, if she found one, then she might be able to help her father.

"No, I haven't seen him shift."

She sighed. "So someone told you he was a dragon shifter and you believed them?"

"No." Simon shook his head and ran his finger around the rim of his cup. "When you meet him, you'll know it. Just as I know it."

"When *I* meet him?" Larisa asked.

"Yes." Simon glanced at his watch. "He'll be here in a couple of hours. When you gave me your flight information, I called him and asked if he'd come and meet you."

"You called him? What is he, your new best friend?" A thrill of excitement prickled across her skin, but she quickly tempered her elation. Simon hadn't seen this guy actually shift. There was no proof he wasn't a liar. They'd met them before. People who claimed to be a shifter but were delusional.

"He wants to help."

"Why?"

"Because we believe that the same person who killed Murray also killed his parents." Simon watched her closely.

"You mean... This dragon shifter is the son of..." She pointed toward the living room where their father slept.

"Yes." Simon nodded. "Ivan was raised in a town called Wishing Moon Bay. He was an orphan and had no idea about any of this."

"Damn." She rested her elbows on the table and threaded her fingers through her hair. Then she looked up at Simon, her lips pursed. "Wait, you said that Murray's daughter is the mate of the dragon shifter's brother?"

"Yes. Fate has a weird sense of humor, doesn't it?" Simon looked up, his attention was drawn to the living room. "Dad's awake."

"I'll go say hi." Larisa cast a critical eye over her brother. "You look as if you need some sleep."

Simon shrugged. "Dad's not the only one who is agitated."

"Did something else happen?" She'd expected Simon to be happier. But instead, he seemed kind of downcast. Perhaps because they now had a new mystery to solve. They'd been so focused on finding the pendant that they had no real plan as to how they were going to use it to track down the dragon shifter who had been responsible for Murray's death and for laying the blame on their dad.

"I did some things I'm not proud of." He stared down at his hands as she waited for him to continue. "Things I regret."

"We all do things we regret," she told him quietly.

"Not like this." He rubbed his hand across his eyes. "Things got out of control."

"Did someone get hurt?" Larisa swallowed hard. This thing had eaten away at her father for decades, would Simon also end up being tormented for his deeds? She'd do whatever it took to stop that from happening.

"We tried to ambush Murray's daughter. She was with her family. We cornered them. At least we thought we did." He raised his eyes to meet hers. "I grabbed Belle." He shook his head and looked away. "It was like things were spinning out of control. I'm not sure what might have happened if someone..." He rubbed the back of his head.

"Are you okay?" Larisa got up from the table and went to her brother. "Did you get hurt?"

"Nothing more than I deserved." He pressed his lips together and grasped her hand as she reached out to touch his head. "Please, I don't deserve your sympathy."

"Listen." She hunkered down next to him. "We're going to get through this together. We'll end this once and for all."

"I hope so." He wrapped his arms around her and hugged her. "Why don't you go see Dad?"

"Okay." She got up and didn't look back as she left the kitchen. Simon hated her seeing him crying and she was certain he was weeping as he got up and gathered the coffee cups.

Her hands balled into fists. What she wouldn't give to get her hands on the person who had done this to them. A dragon shifter. Her nostrils flared. As much as she wanted to meet a dragon shifter in real life, she had little time for them. From what they'd learned about dragons over the years, they weren't the nicest of people.

Except Andor. He'd been her father's friend. According to her father, he had a big heart and whereas most dragon shifters hoarded their wealth, Andor had used it to help others. Larisa wished she'd met him, but she'd been born after Andor was killed and after her father had changed.

"Hi, Dad." Larisa smiled brightly as she entered the living room and went to her father who lay staring at the window with unseeing eyes.

"Larisa." He blinked several times before he turned his head and focused on her face. "When did you get here?"

"I just arrived. You were sleeping and I didn't want to disturb you." She went to him, her jaw tense as she fought to keep her emotions under control. What she wouldn't give for her dad to be happy. To see him smile. To see him free of the fear that seemed to have taken hold of him more and more, over the last decade.

"It's good to see you, Larisa. I've missed you." He clutched her hand and squeezed it just like he used to do when she was a little girl in need of comfort.

"It's good to be home." It wasn't a lie. She was happy to be home even though there was such uncertainty surrounding them. Whenever she was away, no matter how much she loved the place she was visiting, her heart always belonged here. Not so much in the house, but with her father.

He'd raised two children single-handedly after their mom died when Larisa was only a baby. Larisa couldn't remember her mom at all, she only recalled her face because of the many photos her dad kept on display. There was no memory of her perfume or the sound of her voice.

Was that a blessing or a curse? It was an eternal debate she'd had over and over, often in the hours when she lay awake in bed staring at the ceiling as she worried about her dad. If her mom were here, things would have been different.

Or not.

Davy Westward would still have been a suspect in a murder case. Those events had happened before Lorraine Westward died. Would she have pulled him out of his misery? Perhaps he would have turned himself into the police and tried to clear his name.

A wave of guilt hit Larisa and she leaned forward and rested her head on his knee.

Davy Westward had never cleared his name because he wouldn't risk being sent to prison. Not when his wife was sick, and his children needed him.

He'd become this shell of a man because of his family.

"Stop blaming yourself," her dad said quietly.

"I'm..."

"I can always tell." He sighed heavily. "None of this was your fault. And we're one step closer to proving my innocence. Thanks to you and your brother."

"Do you trust the dragon shifter?" she asked.

"I do." He stroked her head, and she closed her eyes as jet lag crept up on her. "He's the son of one of the best men I ever knew."

She raised her head and stared into her father's eyes. "You're sure."

He smiled, his eyes lighting up as he held her gaze. "I'm certain. He looks just like him."

"Then I can't wait to meet him." She rested her head back on her dad's knee.

She wanted to trust Ivan, too. But dragon shifters had only brought misery to their family. Not always with intent.

But misery all the same. Why would this one be any different?

IVAN

"Thanks for driving me." Ivan stared out of the window as Zara drove toward Davy Westward's house. Simon had called Ivan a couple of days ago and asked if he'd come and meet his sister, Larisa, so they could discuss the pendant.

As if we haven't discussed the pendant enough, his dragon answered.

"You're welcome," Zara replied and side-eyed Karros, her mate.

We're a little old for babysitters, his dragon's amused tone was combined with an eye-roll.

They mean well, Ivan told him, and his hand closed around the backpack on the seat next to him. Ever since a piece of his dragon treasure had been found, his family had been acting weird around him, as if he needed protecting.

They have been acting weird! His dragon laughed. Have you seen us lately?

We have it under control now, Ivan replied. With the help of Fiona and her family, he'd gotten used to having the treasure around. It still called to him, it was still a part of him, but it no longer controlled him.

We no longer experience the need to tear someone's head from their shoulders if they touch it. His dragon chortled. Such uncontrollable urges. No wonder Zara and Karros are accompanying us back to Wishing Moon Bay. They're probably worried we'll murder someone if they come too close to our pack.

Not going to happen. I could give it away now and I'd be fine, Ivan said easily.

Liar. His dragon settled down and curled his tail around his head, covering his eyes. I'm not sure what else the Westwards want from us. We don't have any more information to give them.

Maybe they like us, his dragon replied. You've seen the way Davy looks at us.

He is certain that the dragon shifter he knew was our father. Ivan's jaw tensed as they neared the house.

It's good to meet someone who knew our parents, his dragon replied.

Ivan touched the door handle, the temptation to yank it open and fly home almost too strong. Yes, it *was* good to meet someone who knew their parents. But at the same time, it tore open old wounds.

That's not why you don't like meeting him, his dragon murmured.

Ivan sighed heavily. His dragon was right. We always hoped that our parents were alive somewhere in the world. If we're really the son of Andor, then all hope of that being true is gone.

Believing they might be alive was a dream. His dragon took a shuddering breath. If they were alive, they would have found their way back to us by now. We always knew we were orphans.

"Is this the house?" Zara's words cut through his thoughts, and he leaned forward.

"Yes, that's the one." He rolled his shoulders and rubbed his face, the car journey had made him sleepy.

"Shall we wait in the car?" Karros asked. "Or we could go grab a coffee and something to eat and meet you back here later."

"No," Ivan replied a little sharply.

"You want us here in case you need to make a quick getaway?" Zara half-turned in her seat to look at him.

"No." He looked down at his hands. "Simon knew you were driving me. He'd like to meet you, too."

"Ah, *Simon*. The man who my sister felled with a tree branch when he attacked Belle." Karros waggled his eyebrows. "I hope he's not going to take it out on me."

"From what I've seen of Simon, he carries that guilt on his shoulders. It was out of character, driven by a desire to help his father." Ivan opened the car door as soon as Zara switched off the engine.

"I guess we all do crazy stuff sometimes." Karros got out of the car and leaned on the door. "If Rift is okay with what happened, since it was his mate who was attacked, then I am willing to move on from it, too."

"Rift is okay with it because Belle is okay with it. If Simon had really hurt her, I don't think things would be that easy." Ivan's hands curled into fists. If Belle had been hurt, Rift wasn't the only one who would be out for revenge. His brothers' mates were part of their family and Ivan would always do whatever it took to protect them.

Karros shut the car door. "It's crazy how all of our lives are mixed up together. Who would have thought that Rift meeting his mate would have led you to that treasure of yours?"

"Why don't you say it a little louder?" Zara glanced around nervously.

"Sorry." Karros looked around. "Is there anyone around we should be worried about? Because Simon wasn't the only one who tried to ambush Belle for the pendant. There were other people with him, too. Maybe they want that tia...*thing* of yours."

"There's no one lurking in the bushes," Zara assured him. "You sure are paranoid."

"I'm not paranoid, I just wish I had your shifter senses," Karros replied.

"And again, why don't you say it a little louder?" Zara aimed a sharp look in his direction.

Karros held up his hands. "Sorry, I am not used to living in the world beyond. I keep forgetting no one knows about all that stuff."

"Let's get inside." Ivan took one last look around before they walked along the street toward the Westward residence.

There's something here, his dragon was alert now, his head raised as he tried to figure out what threat might be lurking among the suburban houses.

Ivan shivered. I sense it, too. But it's not like anything I've ever sensed before.

Is this some kind of magic? His dragon bristled at the thought and his tail swished from side to side like Rift's snow leopard when he got angry.

Maybe Karros was right, and the Westwards have set us up. They want the tiara.

Or me. His dragon stood alert, ready to break free if they were attacked.

"Ivan." Zara touched his shoulder lightly and he jumped as if he'd been jabbed with a hot poker. "Are you okay?"

"Yeah." He ran a shaky hand through his hair. "It's just..."

She tilted her head to one side and stared at him, her eyes narrowing before widening. "Your mate is close."

"What?" His forehead furrowed but she was right. Of course she was right.

Ivan straightened up and pushed his senses out, trying to locate her. She had to be close.

"You made it!" Simon appeared from around the side of the house and came to meet them.

"We did." Ivan breathed in deeply, drawing on lessons Fiona had given him on how to control himself around his treasure. He let the breath out and arched an eyebrow at Zara, who was still staring at him.

Our mate is more precious than any treasure. His dragon relaxed a little. But not much.

"Thanks for coming." Simon lowered his voice and looked toward the house.

Ivan immediately pushed his senses in that direction. How many people were in the house, was there an ambush waiting for them? Perhaps they had done something to Ivan to make him feel as if his mate was close.

Or perhaps they had found more of his treasure?

"I'm Zara." Zara stepped in front of Ivan, giving him a moment to compose himself as he fought off another wave of intense emotions. "And this is Karros, Elise's brother."

"Oh." Simon hesitated and put his hand to the back of his head. "She sure has some upper body strength."

"Tell me about it." Karros offered his hand to Simon. "She knows how to handle herself. No hard feelings."

Simon shook his head as he took Karros's hand. "None at all. I deserved it. I don't know what came over me. All I could think about was my dad."

"We do what we have to, to protect our family." Karros glanced sideways at Ivan. "Shall we go inside?"

"Sure. My sister arrived a couple of hours ago. We've prepared some food if you're hungry?" Simon led them toward the house.

"You know shifters are always hungry." Karros earned another wary look from Zara.

"Good, there's plenty of food." He led them around the side of the house, with each step Ivan became more aware of his mate. She was there, so close, but he didn't want to stumble into the kitchen like some lovesick fool. He needed to keep it together.

Aren't we going to tell her she's our mate? His dragon wasn't happy with that idea.

Of course we'll tell her. I just don't want her first impression of us to be... Well, we both know what happened with our brothers. We're a dragon shifter, we should at least try to keep our composure.

True, each of our brothers has, so far, made a fool of themselves when they first meet their mate.

Zara and Karros kept glancing at him as Simon opened the kitchen door and stepped inside. "This is my sister, Larisa. And my dad, Davy." He introduced his family, who were seated around the kitchen table.

Ivan had already met Davy a couple of times, they'd spoken about the pendant and the events surrounding it ending up in Murray's hands. They'd also spoken a little about the dragon shifter whose death had set a chain reaction in motion that had affected so many lives.

The dragon shifter who Davy was convinced was his father.

"Good to meet you." Zara stepped forward, covering for Ivan who was frozen to the spot for a long moment. "I'm Zara. And this is Karros."

"Hi." Karros raised his hand.

"You're fae?" Larisa stood up and leaned forward, looking at Karros's slightly pointed ears, half-hidden under his shoulder-length hair.

"I am." Karros brushed his hair back behind his ears. "Am I the first fae you've ever met?"

"You are." Larisa lifted her hand as if she longed to touch his ears to make sure they were real and they weren't just glued on.

"Go ahead." He moved closer and leaned his head toward her.

"Are you sure it isn't a bit weird?" She reached out to him, and her fingertips brushed the tips of his ears. "Amazing."

"Thanks." Karros grinned and arched an eyebrow at Zara.

"He doesn't need his head to get any bigger." Zara nudged Karros in the ribs, and he chuckled as he moved away, leaving Ivan facing his mate.

"And you must be the dragon shifter." A shy smile crossed her lips as she met his eyes. "Although, it's not as easy for you to prove what you are."

Damn, she was beautiful. With light blue almond-shaped eyes and a heart-shaped face, framed by silver-blonde hair, she reminded him of the elven race, a mythical people who used to live in the fae realm.

"I..." He opened his mouth to say more but his brain seemed to have become disengaged.

"And I thought I would be the one staring." She tilted her head to one side. "Wow, your eyes..."

Ivan blinked. "Sorry."

Her smile softened and heat spread across her skin, turning her cheeks pink. "Don't apologize. You're truly unique."

"So are you." Heat built inside him and his eyes flashed amber as he burned with need for her.

You should tell her, his dragon insisted.

Not yet, Ivan answered. This isn't the time.

He knew it deep in his soul. Just as he knew his life would never be the same again.

Ivan might be able to control his desire for his treasure, but he was never going to be able to control his desire for his mate.

She was more a part of him than any gold or jewels.

Printed in Great Britain
by Amazon

62356086R00143